BANGOR MAINE MURDERS

By

Elvis Noble

A Club Lighthouse Publishing Book

ISBN 978-1-77217-329-1

A Club Lighthouse Horror Edition

Table of Contents

CHAPTER ONE
"ENTRANCE"

ERIC BANE, A TEN-YEAR veteran of the Bangor Police Department, sat on a piece of driftwood at Cascade Park. With his modest six foot one and one hundred and six five pounds, he took a sip of grape soda reflecting his approach to the newest murder scene. *Hmm, this case is a classic 'who done it' type of murder. I do believe the evidence will need to speak for the victims,* he pondered. He gave off a big BURP! walking up to his classic 1969 Dodge Charger with its beautiful candy apple metallic silver color. As he got in the driver's seat, his cell phone rang. He looked at the date on his watch as he answered the phone; it was May 15, 2001.

"Detective Eric Bane, how can I help you?"

"You'd better get your ass down the crime scene before I pull out a can of whoop ass on you."

"OK chief, you don't need to be an asshole about it."

Eric hanged up his cell phone then turned the car over. He loved to hear it purr as he peeled out of his private spot to reflect and recharge for any new case. The chief texted him the address for the new crime scene. *This case is totally new, I'm going to take a different approach than any of my other cases while on the force,* he pondered and reflected as he pulled up to 8416 Haven Street. The crime scene itself appeared to be in a very low crime area of Bangor. Eric walked up, showed his shield then walked into a very gruesome sight. He directed everyone out for a few moments to allow him to study then make up his own opinion on the case.

The smell of dried blood gave him a strong desire to throw up in his mouth. Eric pulled out a small flashlight to study each body. The first body was a female around fifty years old and a bit on the chubby side. Her mouth was gaping open with a look of extreme terror. Eric removed the sheet to better view the body. Right away, he noticed evidence of a sexual assault. Dried blood had seeped from the anal and vaginal area of her body prior to expiring. There were no stab wounds. There was a single gunshot wound to the right side of her temple. He looked for stab wounds or any other defensive wounds and none were found. The female looked to be around a plump two hundred and ninety pounds. Her long black hair, which looked like it hadn't been combed in a week was caked in blood. Her eyes looked like two lumps of coal, which matched her black hair. The scent of stale sex gave him another reason to lose his appetite. Eric put the sheet back over the body as a show of the respect for the dead. He noticed her purse on the floor on the left side of the bed. Eric quickly put on rubber gloves then pulled out her wallet. Casey Williams born February 5, 1951.

He then looked on the other side of the bed only to find what appeared to be the husband. His head shaved bald with a very bushy goatee didn't have many defensive wounds. As with the prior victim, there was only a gunshot wound to the temple on his right side. He looked to be a very slender man of around one hundred and twenty-five pounds. The male victim's eyes were as blue as the ocean on the eve of a morning tide. Eric looked down then noticed his penis had been severed then placed by his head. He also noticed that the male had defecated prior to his death. Lying on the nightstand, Eric found his wallet then quickly pulled out his driver's license. Matt Williams, born August 16, 1951. Something told him to look in the living room. The floor creaked as he made his way then noticed a young twenty-year-old female. The young female looked like she had seen a ghost. Her mouth gaped open with dried semen caked on her lips. She noticed the young woman's long black hair caked in her own blood. Just like the first female victims there was caked blood on both the anal and vaginal parts of this young woman's body. She looked to be no more than five feet two in height. *Hmm... the CSI team already had samples of all the evidence but no murder weapon. There are no signs of forced entry into the house, which means the assailant was known to the Casey family. There are three victims, which classifies this as a serial killer. It's time to use my special gift that no one knows I have,* Eric thought as he rubbed his chin in deep thought. He also noticed a mask of a vampire with a sinister smile lying by the young woman's body.

After taking a cleansing breath, Eric walked back to the first victim then grasped her hand. Little did anyone know that he could view memories of the victim. He subtly closed his eyes to see what she saw prior to death.

A FREAKISH MOMENT LATER, Eric found himself in the bedroom. He quickly found cover with the neighboring curtain to avoid detection. Right away, he noticed Casey kissing her husband Matt then turning off the light to go to sleep. Matt did the same then curled up close to his wife. Moments, later small subtle steps came from the distance. Two females came into the room silently. The first woman looked to be a beefy six foot two and around one hundred and sixty pounds. Her eyes, brown and dark coldly stared at Casey. Eric noticed that she took off her clothes exposing her bodacious breasts. He looked down then his mouth gaped open in surprise. This woman had both genitals. She had a penis as big as a horse. There was also a vaginal area. *A hermaphrodite for a serial killer, what the hell!* Eric said to himself.

Then suddenly the vision ended leaving him sitting in a chair. He heard a knock on the door. The coroner's office had arrived to take all the bodies for autopsy. He quickly left the murder scene then walked back to his car. The coroner's office swiftly removed the bodies as Eric watched from a distance. Just as he was about to get into his car, he noticed a very goth looking woman wearing a shield on her belt walking to up him. He noticed right away she looked to be no more than four foot eleven with blond hair bound tightly in a pony tail in the back of her head. Her eyes were as green as spring meadow on a subtle Bangor Maine morning.

"Detective Eric Bane, how are you?"

"Who in the hell are you? I haven't seen you at the office at all."

"That's because I was just transferred from Miami Florida to your department. My name is Allie Phillips, also a detective."

"That still doesn't explain why you're here?"

"Chief Harry Montel assigned me to this case along with you. I've viewed the evidence that's been emailed to me. What did you figure out while you were at the Williams Family crime scene?"

"This really pisses me off. Harry knows that I like to work alone. It's where I do my best work."

"The chief told me you would act this way. So tough shit, you and I have now become partners going forward."

"I've classified this a serial murder. Once they kill three that takes the classification up to serial. My gut tells me it's also a sex crime. How about you?"

"The coroner's office emailed my cell. It appears preliminary results show sexual fluids of both female and male. It's his opinion that they may have two killers?"

"Wanna go to Ed's Burgers for a bite to eat?"

"Are you hitting on me, sir? If you feed me, do you expect more from me?"

"Don't be silly, it's just my way of getting to know you."

"I wouldn't have a problem if you were. I don't have a car. Can we take yours to the Ed's?"

"Sure jump in. I'll drive us there."

Allie got in the passenger side then put her seatbelt on. Eric got in then turned the car over. A smile came over his face. He liked the hear his car purr like a satisfied kitten after drinking its milk. He peeled rubber then they headed to Ed's Burgers. As he drove, out of the corner of his eye, he noticed Allie staring at his crotch. He also noticed her nipples becoming erect as she continued to stare. *I wonder if he has a horse sized cock?* Allie asked herself as she felt moist in her jeans. Twenty minutes later they made it to the restaurant. Allie watched him park then get out of the car to open the door for her. As he walked toward the building, she was staring at his butt. They were able to get a table right away. Both of them ordered a cheeseburger deluxe with grape soda, which seemed to be Eric's favorite meal. She smiled as the waitress brought them their meal. Eric had a slight smile on his face. Allie wasted no time in taking a hulking side bite of her burger. He smiled then did the same.

"I've also read in the report that the killers left a mask of a vampire, which seems to be his or her signature."

"I've noticed that too. With the semen found the dirtbag sexually assaulted the young female, which pisses me off a lot."

"I totally get it and understand. The shot to the temple of each victim also appears they have a signature developing here."

"I would agree. What's the next step in the case?"

"The only problem that I have is developing a profile. I don't know if the killer is male or female. Yet the fluids show both. It's means that the case is a little complicated."

"Allie, we need to be transparent here. I have a gift that I want to show you to see what I've discovered.

You need to keep this private and confidential if I do it."

"Then show me your gift. I admit, you have me a bit intrigued.

He reached over to grab her hand then closed his eyes. They both appeared in the room where Eric had the vision. He quickly found cover with the neighboring curtain to avoid detection. Right away, he noticed Casey kissing her husband Matt then turning off the light to go to sleep. Matt did the same then curled up close to his wife. Moments, later small subtle steps came of the distance. Two females came into the room silently. The first woman looked to be a beefy six foot two and around one hundred and sixty pounds. Her eyes, brown and dark coldly stared at Casey. Eric noticed that she took off her clothes exposing her bodacious breasts. He looked down then his mouth gaped open in surprise. This woman had both genitals. She had a penis as big as a horse. There was also a vaginal area. *A hermaphrodite for a serial killer, what the hell!* Eric said to himself. Then suddenly the vision ended leaving him sitting in a chair. He heard a knock on the door. Eric then opened his eyes to find Allie with her mouth gaping open showing an awe-struck expression on her face.

"This is some mind-blowing shit. You've discovered our main killer is a hermaphrodite. Listen I also have a secret to show you also. You must keep my secret in strict confidence."

"What's your secret Allie?"

"I don't want to tell you. I want to show you. Let's finish up our burgers then drive back to Cascade Park. I need to be in the water to show you. Are you game,

Eric?"

He raised his eyes in wonderment. They quickly finished their burgers. Eric used his debit card to pay for their meal. In haste, they both got in his car then quickly drove to Cascade Park. Thirty minutes later they made it to his favorite spot then he parked the car. They both got out then stared at each other.

"Are you ready to see my secret?"

"Yeah, please show me."

Allie smiled then she shed her shirt and bra exposing her big bodacious breasts. She then took her jeans and panties off then bent over toward Eric. He instantly popped a big boner, which made her smile. She briskly walked toward then end of the dock with him following right behind her. Allie ran then jumped into the air heading toward the water. Right before she hit the water, her legs vanished then a long fin appeared as she hit the water. She went underwater then came back up. Eric noticed right away, her eyes changed into a golden color and that she had gills on each side of her neck. She swam up to the dock to strike up a conversation with him.

"Wow, that is also some mind-blowing shit! You're a mermaid!"

"You're a familiar. A person that can see with the eyes of a murder victim. That's also very cool. Please keep this a secret."

"Don't worry, your secret is safe with me."

She jumped high in the air then back on the dock. Right before landing her legs reappeared then she was standing there naked right in front of him. Allie smiled as she noticed the raging bulge in his jeans.

"I can help you out with that if you like. Also, I don't have a place to stay. Can I stay with you until I find myself an apartment or house to rent?"

"Sure, if you don't have a problem with a bachelor pad."

They walked back then she found her clothes then got dressed again. In the back of his mind, he was thinking Allie could prove to be a solid asset and also help him with such a bizarre case. Eric and Allie made it to the car then he noticed that she also had something else to disclose to him. They both leaned on the Charger. Eric, being the gentlemen that he is, pulled out two ice cold cans of grape soda then handed her one.

"You're reading my mind. My throat is parched and could use something wet to help me."

"I'm also realizing that you have something else to disclose to me, don't you? Also, you're welcome roomie."

"Eric, you're right, I do have something to tell you but again, what I'm about to tell you is a secret and must never to be disclosed that it exists. The same would apply to me being a mermaid. This guy that I'm about to tell you about has been fighting crime here in Bangor Maine as long as it's been in existence."

CHAPTER TWO
"ESSENCE OF PREY"

Eric AND ALLIE GOT into his car then headed back to his house. She wanted to make herself at home to continue to work on the case. As they pulled in with the Charger, Allie's eyes got as big as silver dollars at what she saw. Eric smiled as he opened her car door. He quickly walked up to the front door of the quaint two-bedroom house that his parents willed to him after their deaths. The door gave off a loud CREEK! as they walked in, Allie's eyes immediately saw a collection of miniature ships from the Civil War. She also noticed old colonial furniture, which she assumed belonged to his parents. She put her nose in the air to smell the ocean mist coming toward the house. Eric also pointed out the stained cherry hardwood floors, which brought a smile to her face. Allie noticed that Eric was a big fan of the ocean and lighthouses. A whole wall showed paintings of several types of shores and lighthouses.

"The house is small, quaint and shows the signs of a bachelor with taste."

"So, you like the house?"

"Of course, I do. Somehow, I knew you were a man of good taste."

"You did mention a third party a while ago. Could you tell me more about that?"

"I have a friend that is a fully vested consultant for the Bangor Police Department. His name is Andros

Surkacksi, a man of Greek decent. What they don't know is that he comes from a three-hundred-year line of vampires. He only feeds on wildlife and never a human. His vampiric powers really come in handy. Andros can only work at night for obvious reasons."

"When can I meet this guy?"

"It's a pleasure to be in your acquaintance, old sport."

Eric jumped about three feet in the air when he noticed a man about six feet six in height. He looked to be a chiseled two hundred and twenty-five pounds. He wore his dark blue-black hair in a pony trail with a very tight braid. His eyes looked like two lumps of coal. Eric stood next Andros, which made him feel small. He pulled out a comb then sleeked his thinning blond hair back.

"You have a very sneaky way to make an appearance, sir."

"You got that right, old sport. My movements are very fast and precise when they need to be."

"Allie tells me that you serve as a consultant for the Bangor Police Department. Would you mind lending Allie and me a hand on this case? Ironically, they are dubbing the murderer as the Vampire Mimic Serial Killer. I only have two questions about you two. How are a very old vampire and a mermaid going to help in the case? What contributing factors can both of you offer this case? Plus, you're a vampire, are you sure that you're not involved in the murders themselves? I would like to hear from each of you as two how you can help me solve this case."

"I'll speak first old sport. I have the power to shapeshift and also do surveillance without getting caught. Of course, I've always had legit warrants from the chief. That's beside the point. I also have a bachelor's degree in criminology and profiling. Plus, since you mentioned a very old vampire. I've only been in Bangor for two hundred years. I came to be a vampire on October fifteenth, fifteen hundred and one in Greece. I'm five hundred years old. So, you if think I'm old, I have a can of whoop ass in my back pocket that tells everyone differently."

"Sounds good to me. I'm sorry if I brought any offense to you Andros."

"None taken old sport. Allie why don't you tell him what you're going to bring to this Vampire Mimic Serial Killer Case."

"As both of you know, I'm a mermaid with special powers. I have the power to read thoughts of any living thing. I speak to all sorts of species all the time. I also have super strength and speed similar to the speed of Andros. One thing that I can also do is the power that separates me from any other living being. I practice white magic. I can astral project myself appearing in two places at once. In closing, Andros and I are both fifth degree black belts in Kung Fu. To speak frankly, both of us can add an extra edge in solving this case."

SUDDENLY, BOTH ANDROS AND Allie

stopped speaking to listen to something that Eric obviously couldn't hear or see. It was so quiet that a person could only hear a pin drop. Andros directed that everyone go out on the deck. His eyes turned completely black. Golden gills made themselves known on each side of Allie's neck. *Something is about to go down,* Eric thought to himself as he walked out with both of them.

"We must go you guys. The hair on the back of my neck is standing straight up. My heightened sense tells me somebody is in trouble."

"What do you mean, Andros?"

"Somebody is in danger. It's my gut feeling that there's going to be another murder."

"Do you know where this is happening as we speak?"

"There is a flooded cave about fifteen miles away from here. If a party can dive there is part of the cave that can be a haven or hiding place for our killers."

"I would agree with you. I'm hearing deafening screams as if somebody is being killed as we speak."

Andros directed them to grasp each arm. Allie went to his left arm. Eric copied her then went to the right arm. Within a split second, everyone ascended in the air. Once they were about one hundred feet in the air, Andros flew towards this cave. Allie's eyes turned into a golden color the closer they got to their destination. Five minutes, later Allie transformed into a mermaid. She shined her eyes toward Andros and Eric. Weirdly, golden gills formed on each side of their throats. Andros pointed to the flooded cave.

"This is where trust needs to take over. Both of you will be able to breath underwater. We have to dive in all at the same time."

Eric had a look of what the hell did I get myself into on his face. Within seconds, a loud SPLASH! came as they dove into the water. Andros and Allie held on to Eric as they swam through the flooded part of the cave. Within seconds they reached the entrance of the cave. Allie's fin vanished then her legs reappeared. Eric had a big look of relief on his face as they quickly and quietly walked to a darkened part of the cave.

"Andros and Allie, you do realize that we can't do anything without a search warrant or even any arrest warrants. All we can really do is just observe," Eric whispered.

"I do realize that we can't do anything old sport. If there is an innocent person that is about to be murdered, with our police powers, we must do your due diligence. Remember, the oath to protect and serve?"

"I understand but please be cautious is all that I'm saying, my friends."

"You got it, old sport."

Eric, Allie and Andros found a bunch of old wooden crates to hide behind. Andros surprised everyone with some portable night goggles. Due to his vampiric powers, he didn't need them. In the distance, they could hear the faint scream of a young girl. Moving like thieves in the night, they got closer and noticed a young woman about the age of twenty-two struggling and screaming, but she had a ball gag, which prevented her from projecting her voice. Eric looked closely then noticed the young woman looked nude with not a stitch of clothing on. There were four poles, both arms and legs were tied with zip ties leaving her defenseless. She looked to be no taller than five foot six and around very lean one hundred and twenty pounds. Allie noticed that she was a ginger. Her hair and pubic area were fire engine red in color. Eric looked a little more closely at the girl. Blood vessels were popping in his head. His eyes turned bloodshot. Andros knew that Eric recognized the girl.

"Do you know who this girl is?" he asked in a very low whisper.

"Yes, she is Angelina Colter. I went to school with her. Before my parents passed, they used to play poker every Friday night with her parents. This case has just become personal to me. Andros, if we're going to make a move, it's got to be pretty damn quick!"

"Don't worry, Andros and I are going to make our move. Eric, you know, we need to identify the killers, right?"

"If she dies, I've got a can of whoop ass for both you in my back pocket."

IN THE DISTANCE THEY noticed a woman around six foot two and one hundred and sixty pounds walking toward the girl. The blond hair that flowed well past her shoulders appeared that she hadn't combed it for weeks. Her body looked butch and chubby. She removed her shirt then bodacious breasts fell out of a skimpy bra. She then pulled off her jogging shorts and panties, exposing a horse sized erect cock with a vaginal area at the base of it. A very skinny small breasted girl that looked like five feet one and around one hundred and five pounds followed her in taking all of her clothes off. She then reached in a bag to put a harness on, then donned a big strap on dildo. The butch woman walked up close to the girl that was tied up. Angelina urinated all over the ground around her. The butch woman laughed manically as she reached into her bag then pulled out a .38 Smith and Wesson pistol with a silencer at the end.

"We need to add this one to the list that we have. She's on the list for the boss. Her whole family is on the list to settle the vendetta our mob boss has with certain people in this whole town. I want to fuck her first then shoot her in the right temple as directed by the mob. Go and get the lube. I'll take the gun and shoot her in the temple. The boss wants me to slice the throat of this one. You know, Katarina Smith, this is a tough thing to do."

"I know, Jody Westshire. Unless you want to be added to the list, we need to get this done then lie low for a while."

Just as Jody cocked the hammer back on the gun to get ready to shoot after raping Angelina, Andros and

Allie jumped into action. Andros moved in nothing but what appeared to be blur, he quickly untied Angelina then ran back into the water with her in tow. Allie jumped then delivered a round house kick to the side of Katarina's head. Also moving in nothing but a blur. A gold ray came from her eyes right onto the pistol held by Jody. She dropped the pistol then Allie jumped in the air then kicked both sides of her head, which knocked her out cold. Allie ran like the wind then grabbed Eric's arm then they ran toward the water. The golden gill reappeared on the side of everyone's throat then they rushed towards the water then swam to freedom. They all entered the water swimming back to the surface as if the devil was chasing them. Allie's legs transformed into a large fin along the way. Everyone made it but then Andros asked for everyone to grab on. He quickly took flight. Allie's large fin vanished then her legs reappeared. Within what seemed to be mere minutes they arrived safely on Eric's deck. He could see a big sigh of relief on everyone's faces as they all calmed down.

"I guess some introductions need to take place here. Angelina Colter, this is Detective Allie Phillips and that huge sized man over there is Special Consultant Andros Surkacksi."

"Very nice to meet you madam."

"Likewise, here, I hope you're OK."

"Once I saw you about to raped and killed, I got stomping mad. The only question that I have for you how your family got involved with the mob? Also, what mob family sent these two bitches here to kill a bunch of our citizens?"

"You know that my dad has a lobster business and a bunch of lobster boats, right?"

"Yeah, what does that have to do with what just happened?"

"My dad was about to lose the whole business to the bank. He fell behind on his loan payments and the bank was about to repossess all of the lobster boats. My dumb father knew a member of the Chicago Mob. His name is Trent Lechesky. He's the son of mafia member Alex Lechesky. They loaned one hundred thousand dollars to my dad to make the loan payments current. In the past six months, the lobster market bottomed out. My dad was unable to make any payments. Trent and his cohorts were sent here to make sure my father and other members of Bangor Maine pay up or lose their lives. My dad may already be dead. I haven't seen him in about five days."

"I've just called the chief and filled him in on this case. He's sending a protective detail to take Angelina to a safe house. The boss also told me that her father Elliot Colter is already at the safe house. Since they are from Chicago, the chief called the feds. They are going to be here in the morning," Allie said as she rubbed Angelina's shoulder to comfort her.

"You realize what you've seen tonight must never to be told to anyone. Our existence must be held in secrecy. That is how we've been able to live among humans. We have the ability to erase the memories completely from your mind."

"I know how the three of you saved me from being raped and killed, I'll forever be in your debt. Don't worry, your secret is safe with me. I'll take it to my grave, that I promise you. Bangor Maine is lucky to have you three serving and protecting their town."

Twenty minutes later, the protective detail assigned by the chief arrived then immediately took Angelina into custody. They promptly left the house as instructed. Andros bade his goodbyes since the sun was coming up. That left Eric and Allie with the house all to themselves. Eric noticed that Allie had a very naughty expression on her face as she walked into the guest bedroom to retire for the night as she shut her door. With his eyes feeling heavy, Eric toddled off to his bedroom to get some well-deserved rest. He took a big gulp of stale grape soda then turned in for the night.

The fresh aroma of French roast coffee wafted toward his bedroom. He could also smell eggs benedict cooking. Eric woke up, took the last gulp of grape soda then got dressed. The aroma of the nectar of the gods was too much for him to take. He walked in to see Allie wearing nothing but a G-string pair of panties and a very skimpy bra. Her boobs looked like they were going to explode out of the bra. She smiled then poured him a cup of coffee then directed him to sit down and enjoy. *Damn! All this all looks yummy including her,* he thought to himself. A big smile came to his face when she also placed a lobster poor boy sub right next to his eggs. With a huge smile, she also brought him a cup of

French roast coffee.

"You better be careful. I just might get used to this. This is a meal fit for a member of royalty and not a man like me."

"If you live with me, you'll be spoiled rotten. As long as I'm part of your dessert."

Eric smiled as he took a bite of his eggs, which down his chin. She smiled big as she took a hulking bite of her own lobster poor boy sandwich. He slurped down a drink of his coffee that had hazelnut creamer mixed in. With coffee dribbling down his chin, he decided it was time to discuss the next steps in the case.

"Have the feds got ahold of you?"

"Yeah, they sent over five agents from the FBI. They are working the angle of the mob part of the case. The chief told me, you and I have jurisdiction in the murder cases. They are going to work the corruption side of the case. They have been after Alex and Trent Lechesky for a long time due to their ties with the mafia. With the money laundering and loans across state lines it will put them away for a very long time. To be honest, it was hard for me to believe that Bangor Police Department still has jurisdiction in the case. The chief made an agreement with them to have a joint hands-off task force. He had a junior deputy bring us arrest warrants for Katarina Smith and Jody Westshire. The cave has been drained. They found five kilos of cocaine, forty-five million in cash. Also found three crates of automatic weapons. The feds were very happy about the recovery of all. As far as Katarina and Jody, their whereabouts are unknown. The chief thinks the mob will be sending more killers until all of the loans are paid in full or the parties involved are all dead."

"With Andros, you and I, our team should be able to find them. It's my gut feeling that this case will take a very long time to solve. We have our work ahead of us. He should be here soon."

"Yeah, I'm updated him on the case. As soon as the sun goes down, he told me he would come and help us develop a plan to find them. Once they're arrested, I'm sure there will be more without a doubt. I hope you didn't mind me using your phone to call him."

"No don't mind at all but we have some time to kill. What would you like to do today?"

"As you know, I'm a mermaid and need to dive to regain my strength. Basically, to recharge my batteries, so to speak. Maybe, we can go out on a date. I found a good steak house on the eastern side of town. Do you want to come and dive with me?"

"I'm always game to try something new. To respond to your other suggestion. Why not, we may have some fun."

"Cool, I'm going to take a quick shower. Why don't you do the same. After that you can drive us to a hidden spot that I use."

"Sounds good to me."

Allie quickly cleaned up the mess from the enhanced breakfast with Eric's help. She quickly scurried into the guest bedroom, which had a dual headed shower. Eric ran into his bedroom that also had a dual headed shower. They both took a quick shower before meeting each other in the kitchen. Allie put on some very loose-fitting sweats with a sweatshirt hoodie on top. He grabbed the keys for the Charger then they walked to the car. Allie had a very content look in her eyes as she got in the driver's side seat. He walked around to the passenger side seat then got in. Eric smiled at Allie as she turned the car over. The Charger purred like a satisfied kitten after having some warm milk.

"To get there, you have to drive east of Bangor. I found a very private and secluded spot to do my dives. Also, I would like you to come with me on the dive. Are you game?"

"Why not? You only live once."

Allie put the pedal to the metal then they drove east of Bangor. Allie opened the window then let the brisk wind hit her hand. Within fifteen minutes, they made it to where she directed. He recognized it right away. It was Bangor Falls National Park. He smiled as he had trouble keeping up with her as she hiked to the spot, she picked out for herself. She showed no hesitation in getting naked right away, which naturally excited Eric. He did the same but couldn't hide his excitement. This made her smile big as she grabbed his hand. Golden gills formed in his neck. They both jumped off a small cliff.

Right before landing in the water, her legs vanished then a large fin took its place. They dove deep into around a seventy-foot drop into the water. Once they landed on the surface, Eric noticed that Allie's eyes glowed brightly with a golden color. A golden aura surrounded her whole body. This made his mouth gape open in wonderment as he continued to watch her. When finished, she directed him to swim up to the surface with her. Allie gave him a thumbs up, which told him she completed the process that she set out to do. They swam up to the surface. Allie bolted out of the water with Eric holding to her hand. While in the air, her fin vanished then her legs reappeared right before they landed in the same spot they dove from. To avoid getting caught, they both got dressed then briskly hiked back to the car.

"So, where do you want to take me on a date?"

"I know of a place just outside of town that makes a killer steak and lobster combo. Are you a white wine or a dark wine girl?"

"I could go for a big steak along with a lobster as big as my forearm. As far as wine, I'm a white wine type of girl. It does have a bad effect on my legs."

"What kind of bad effect?"

"It makes me open them," she said with a seductive smile.

Eric, with big boyish grin, opened the door for Allie then shut her door. He turned the car over then listen to it purr. In a lot of ways, listening to his car purr made him feel secure. To show off for Allie, he put the pedal to the metal leavings nothing but dust in their wake. The restaurant itself was on the total opposite side of Bangor.

It was his hope that they would still be open. The owner used to also play poker with his dad on the same night as Angelina and her parents. Thirty minutes later, they pulled into The Anchor Bay Steak and Lobster House. Eric pulled up and the valet attendant met them at the car. The attendant greeted both of them with a smile. He took Allie by the hand then they walked into the entrance of Anchor Bay. The owner, Roy Olderstein, greeted them with a huge smile. He walked with a limp due to having a car accident years ago.

With his five-foot five small frame and around one hundred twenty-five-pound body, he made sure they got the best seat in the house. Located right next to the water. The tide would come in and also shoot mist through the screen of the window. Roy's wife Zelda brought the menu to them. Allie's eyes grew as big as silver dollars when she noticed they had a huge piece of prime rib on the menu. A gleam came over her face as she ordered it with a side of steamed broccoli. Eric ordered the same due to his love of prime rib. Roy also added two huge Maine lobsters for them to also enjoy. They brought a big garden salad to enjoy. Eric engulfed his with some ranch dressing. Allie, ironically, also loved ranch. They both seemed to complement each other. After they finished their salad, two huge pieces of prime rib came to them piping hot with minced garlic and the natural juices from the prime rib itself. Zelda brought a vintage bottle of white wine. She figured that a 1988 bottle would do the trick.

CHAPTER THREE
"WOLFEN"

ERIC QUICKLY FOUND A cork screw to open the bottle of wine. Allie's eyes beamed with great joy as a loud POP! sound came from the bottle. Eric smelled the cork, which is customary to see if the wine was still palatable. He graciously poured Allie wine glass first then he poured his own. She had a look of love in her eyes as they subtly and softly hit their wine glasses together. Allie was the first to cut a hulking chunk of her prime rib in the *au jus*. Her eyes rolled back in a carnivore's delight. Eric was the second to do the same. By both of their plates stood a huge Maine lobster just aching to be eaten. Zelda and her crew had already cracked the shells. Next to that stood hot butter and lemon. Not being shy at all, Allie cut off a big chunk of her lobster. With steam rolling off of it, she dipped it into the hot butter then squeezed a bunch of lemon juice on it. Eric laughed at her due to butter dribbling down her chin.

He noticed that Allie had a beaming look in her eyes during the course of the meal. Thirty minutes later, they finished the meal then poured a couple of glasses of wine. Eric had to watch because he had to drive. After they finished, he used his debit card to pay the tab. Allie made sure he was generous with the tip. Eric grabbed her by the hand as they made their way to the Charger. Before he could even react, Allie grabbed his crotch then French kissed him. This naturally got him very excited. A few moments later, he opened the door then put a very tipsy Allie in the passenger seat of the car. Before Eric made it the car, he jumped about three feet in the air when Andros snuck up on him.

"You need to stop doing that!"

"Old sport, I have some good news and some bad news. What do you want to hear first?"

By the time, Allie sobered up then got out the car to be part of the conversation. Eric grabbed her by the hand. They both leaned on the hood of the car in preparation of his message.

"Let's start with the good news first," Allie said as she grabbed Eric's leg in a teasing way.

"After I'd been informed that the arrest warrants were approved, when it got dark, I immediately went on a hunt for Katarina Smith and Jody Westshire. For the last couple of hours, they were nowhere to be found. Then I found them."

"What's the bad news?"

"Old sport, instead of telling you, I want you and Allie to grab my hands then you'll see what I found."

Nervously, Allie grabbed his left hand then Eric grabbed his right hand. Their breathing lessened and their hearts began to beat rapidly. Beads of sweat ran Eric's forehead as he closed his eyes. Allie's head was already drenched in sweat. She had a look of get on with it on her face. She then closed her eyes. Andros did the same.

IN A SPLIT SECOND, Andros, Allie and Eric appeared in a secluded part of Bangor Falls National

Park. Very close to where Allie did her dives. Andros directed them to follow him then hide behind a grove of trees. Jody Westshire had a vagrant man stripped nude with his hand tied to two poles. Katarina Smith tied a rope around his neck then walked away forcing him to bend over. Jody put a ball gag in his mouth to lessen his chances of screaming and calling for help. She took her top off and her bodacious breasts fell out. Each nipple stood on end in anticipation. Allie saw the bulge in Jody's jeans, which she took off exposing the horse sized cock on top of a very moist vaginal area. This gave Allie a strong desire to throw up in her mouth. Eric also felt very green gilled seeing this happening first hand.

"This one is a freebie for the mob. I need to get my nut on. Also, please get the pistol ready."

"You go girl!" Katarina yelled with a supportive tone.

Suddenly, Andros eyes turned the complete color of black. Long blood-soaked fangs came out from each side of his mouth. Three distinct blood vessels in his forehead made themselves visible.

A long SNAP! POP! and breaking from branches came out. Four indigenous men jumped out of the air then as they landed their bodies began to morph into wolves. Due to his studies in high school and college, Eric recognized each tribe. The first one to complete the transformation into a wolf was an Abenaki tribal member. A loud scream came out of his mouth then all of his limbs turned onto paws. His hand turned into massive claws. Right before completing the transformation his eyes turned into the color of blood.

The second to complete the same transformation into a wolf was a Micmac tribal member. The third one to complete the same transformation into a wolf was a Passamaquoddy tribal member. The fourth and final member to complete the transformation into a wolf was a Penobscot tribal member. Eric concluded all of them were members of the Wabanaki Nation.

It got deathly quiet. All a person could hear was their own heartbeat. The first two tribal members salivated as they jumped high in the air. Long fangs came out of their mouths along with large razor-sharp claws out of their paws as they lunged toward Jody Westshire. A loud CLICK! came out as the two wolves made contact with her body. With one swipe the wolves cut Jody's body exactly in half. Blood squirted high into the air then landed into their gaping mouths. One of them bit her face off while the other ate her intestines. A loud POP! SNAP! rang out as they each took a leg bone then ran off like thieves in the night.

The last two tribal members salivated as they jumped high in the air. Long fangs came out of their mouth along with large razor-sharp claws out of their paws as the lunged toward Katarina Smith. A loud CLICK! came out as the two wolves made contact with her body. With one swipe the wolves cut Katarina exactly in half. Blood squirted high into the air then into their gaping mouths. One of them bit her face off, while the other ate her intestines. A LOUD POP! SNAP! rang out as they each took a leg bone then ran off like thieves in the night. The vagrant defecated on himself while breaking free. This was due to horrifying murders he just witnessed.

As he ran off in the distance, a very big tomahawk hit this man in the chest. The four tribal members transformed back into their human indigenous form. One of the them used a sharp knife to castrate this man then gobbled up his genitals. Another used a sharp knife to scalp him. With the large tomahawk one of them sliced his head in two. Each side rolling to the right then to the left. A huge spurt of blood shot high in the air as all of them had their mouths gaping to enjoy the taste of human blood. All of their pupils were the pure and sinister color of blood. All of them ran off in the distance like thieves in the night.

ALLIE AND ERIC BROKE free from Andros's thoughts then immediately bent over A vomit shot out from their mouths like wild fire, expelling all the wonderful food they had just had on their date.

"Judging by how you saw me transform. Vampires and werewolves are sworn enemies. What you saw isn't normal even for a werewolf. All four of these tribal members suffer from what's called Blood Rage. In a nutshell, they are sociopathic and have no regard for human life."

"Seeing this vision was one of the most horrifying and brutal things that I've ever witnessed. Maybe it's for the best that Katarina and Jody are out of the picture. That way they won't be able to terrorize any more of the citizens of Bangor Maine."

"I'd agree with you whole heartily but our team is now threatened by a bunch of werewolves that are infected with Blood Rage. To add insult to injury the mob sent more of their teammates to either recover the money or have them pay with their lives. There are too many of them. My contact at the airport said the Chicago Syndicate sent twelve team members who just arrived. The reason they know about it is by using facial recognition software. All twelve of them have records and ties to the mafia. There are six women and six men that've been sent to us. My sixth sense tells me they have the same orders from their bosses from the mafia. The six men are loners from the Italian Mob based on Sicily Italy, old sport."

"How in the hell are we going to fight against this? Also, excuse my language but this is pretty fucked up. Eric and I just had a wonderful romantic date with a beautiful array of food. I'm a little pissed at you!" she said with a look of distaste toward Andros."

"Yeah, I'm also very angry at you. I'm really getting close to my girl then you had to go and fuck it up."

"I'm sorry, old sport my apologies. We need to make some decisions as to how to approach this case. One thing I do know. The signatures of the killers are all going to be the same. The mob can be compared to locusts. You kill a bunch of them then a hundred more come in their place. So, in conclusion, we need to make some decisions quickly and decisively. The chief told me because of what's happen in the case, we have free reign or blanket warrants, which will be authorized on anything we need to bring this case to a close."

"My gut is telling that we're going to need protection. Allie has special powers but they are no match against what's before us. We're a team of three.

It's like a David verses Goliath, if you know what I mean. I've grown close to Allie. I'll make it my main mission if I have to do so. Andros, do you have any friends that we can all upon for protection? Also, to assist us in the stroke building type of case."

"Yeah, old sport.   Do you remember the old abandoned farm about three miles from your house?"

"Yes, it used to belong to my dad's widowed brother. His wife died of cancer then he passed away from cancer year ago. Why do you ask?"

"My family purchased all of the land from the bank. I have five brothers and one sister that are all like me. They only feed on nearby wildlife. My father is also there. The chief has given them all temporary police powers. My father has also conversed with the vampire council in Greece. They are also going to send more reinforcements if needed, old sport."

"What about the werewolves that you encountered from the Wabanaki Nation?"

"My sixth sense told me you would ask about that. Believe or not, in Greece four members of the council of vampires are werewolves that have signed a blood pact with our family never to bring harm and have sworn to protect our kind and also their own. My father told me that they are flying to Greece as we speak. The four members and some of their extended family will help us exterminate the corrupted line in the Wabanaki Nation. Werewolves are just like us. They want to live among humans and keep their identity in the utmost secrecy. That's how are we've been to exist in the forever changing world, old sport."

CHAPTER FOUR
"BLENDING OF
THREE"

"IT'S HIGH TIME THAT Eric and I recharge our batteries. We're going to go back in The Anchor Bay Steak and Lobster House and order the same but we're going to have them deliver it to Eric's house. He and I are going to take a hot shower together and enjoy some food. We've seen enough blood and gore to last us a life time.

"If my opinion holds any weight. Andros, keep all of your family close by us for protection. You'll need to work close with us going forward. As far as how we are going to deal with the Wabanaki Nation? Have your father call upon all of the members of the council including the werewolf members to please come to help us and protect us. The case itself is dubbed Vampire Mimic Serial Killers. Eric, you and myself will close this case. My mindset is the bigger they are, the harder they fall."

Roy and Zelda Olderstein heard the last of conversation when it applied to the dinner they lost. With a smile, Zelda directed the chef to whip the same exact meal along with the white wine. One of Roy's drivers took the food out of the restaurant then peeled out with his 1969 Ford Truck and headed to Eric's house.

This prompted Eric to get Allie into the passenger

side seat. He graciously opened the door for her then shut it like a complete gentleman for her. Andros quickly piled into the back seat. Eric jumped in the driver's seat then turned the Charger over. Hearing the engine purr like a kitten soothed his already frayed nerves from what Allie and he had experienced. Nothing but dust came over as they left the parking lot. Andros smiled but had a death grip on the seats. She had a great big smile on her face as they promptly pulled into his own driveway with Roy's driver at the ready to bring the food into the house. Allie directed the driver to promptly place all the good on the kitchen table. She tipped a driver a twenty dollar bill then he took off in his truck as if the devil were chasing him. Andros and Allie were up to something. Eric's sixth sense seemed to tell him they were both up to something. Just they got into the house, Andros shut the door quickly. Allie snapped their fingers then all three of them vanished to an unknown location. Eric looked at his watch then noticed time stood still.

Moments later all of them arrived in the barn of the Andros family farm. An older looking version of Andros walked into the barn then sat down. *Hmm I wonder if that's his father,* Eric said to himself trying to remain calm. By appearance, he looked to be around six foot seven and around two hundred and fifty pounds of chiseled muscles bulging out of his clothes. This strange man also had his salt and pepper hair in a tight ponytail in the back of his head. Andros decided to break ice and introduce his family.

"Eric Bane, this is my father, Victor Surkacksi."

"Glad to meet you sir. The honor is all mine."

"Please be seated, we have a lot to discuss here."

ERIC FOLLOWED VICTOR'S REQUEST then held Allie's hand nervously. Suddenly a man around seven feet tall walked into the room. The ground shook as he walked forward toward Eric and Allie. He wore a crown on top of his head. His hair that looked as white as snow flowed down well past his shoulders. His eyes were golden and he also had a golden aura beaming from his body. The eyes of this man showed wisdom, love and consideration. This stranger also walked with a huge blinding trident in his left hand. *This is a dead giveaway. It has to be Allie's father or some relation to her,* Eric silently thought to himself.

"I can hear your thoughts my son. Please be calm and put your soul at ease. I'm known by many names such as Poseidon or King Neptune. King of the Sea. Yes, Allie is my daughter. You'll need to have my permission to mate with her. Permission is granted but you'll need to listen to all of these men that you're about to meet. You can call me Ned for short. Is that clear young man?"

"Crystal clear sir, again the honor is all mine."

Suddenly, huge KNOCK! came to the barn door. The ground shook like an earthquake. Allie and Eric both squeezed each other's hands tightly as a huge creature walked inside the barn. A huge THUD! came from each of his steps. As he made his appearance, Eric looked at him with a little bit of fear in his eyes. He dwarfed all of the others. He stood a huge eight foot two and well over five hundred pounds in weight. *If this is his human form, I would hate to see what he transforms into,* Eric thought to himself but he got a glare from Ned. Telling him to respect and listen to all in attendance communicated telepathically directly to him.

Victor got up to address those in attendance.

"Ladies and Gentlemen, I would like to introduce you to a very old friend of mine. This is Louis Anderstiene, one of founding members of the vampire council in Greece. As a show of respect, he doesn't need to transform into a werewolf. Without any doubt in anybody's mind, he is not only a werewolf but he is also our blood brother. All in attendance, please address him as Big Lou. This is per his request."

"Thank you for your respect, Victor. I'm Big Lou," he with a booming voice that sounded like it came from the heavens.

"Ned, please take charge of this meeting sir," Victor said as he bowed to him as a show of respect and brotherhood.

"Thank you, Victor. As you know, Mr. Eric Bane, my daughter Allie and Andros are up against some very unfair odds. We all discussed an idea that in the history of Creation has never been done before. All of us are going to create a hybrid that no one has ever seen before. If he accepts this, Eric will become a very powerful creature. He'll need to use prudence, restraint and a high regard for human life. He'll be part mermen, part vampire and last but not least part werewolf. He'll have the powers and privileges of each species. To feed the vampire in him, he'll feed on nearby wildlife. such as deer, elk, bear. To feed the werewolf inside of him, he'll feed strictly on cattle. In conclusion, to feed the mermen inside of him and to retain his special telepathic power, he'll have to dive with Allie every forty-eight hours for the rest of eternity. Eric, if you accept this offer, Victor will pass on the vampire gene to you by biting you in the left side of the neck. Big Lou will pass on the werewolf gene to you by biting on the right side of the neck. I'll pass on the mermen gene by using my trident in your chest. Eric, you'll never be asked or forced to decide but based on circumstance, speak yeah or nay. This is the only time this will ever be offered. In conclusion, you must accept this offer of your own volition."

"If it's for the betterment of humanity then I'm all for it. Will I become immortal?"

"Yes, some of the people among you are over five hundred years old. So, what does that tell you, my son?"

"That would be an abundant yes. Please make this happen."

Andros grabbed Eric by the hand then placed him standing between Big Lou and Victor. Ned stood right in front of him holding his trident. With lightning like speed, Big Lou bit the right side of Eric's neck slightly drinking some of his blood with reverence and respect. Victor bit Eric on the left side of his neck. Slightly drinking a little of his blood. Ned's trident shined brighter than anything witnessed by the eyesight of any creature. He gently forced the trident into Eric's chest. Within seconds his body went limp to die a mortal death.

"When I snap my fingers, Andros, Allie and Big Lou will be with Eric in his house. Andros, you'll stand guard until he comes to from the exchange of DNA. Please cross train him as much as possible."

Ned snapped his fingers then Andros, Allie and Big Lou appeared back in Eric's room. Big Lou and Allie gently place his lifeless body on his bed.

"If he survives, he'll be one of the most powerful creatures out there," Big Lou said as he looked over Eric's body with hopeful eyes.

"It's my hope that he does comes back, he's such a genuine soul. To me, he is very selfless and analytical when it comes to his work."

"This whole situation is involving the mob, and blood rage infected werewolves. The danger level is very high. One thing that you don't know about the transformation is that we've installed him with memories and knowledge. It will not take much training at all. Andros is nearby and can assist. So will I be here but like I said there won't need much training."

"Is there a chance that he won't come back?"

"Yes, there is. This experiment has never been done. We mixed the DNA of the three species. His body is going to either reject it and shut down. Or it will mix together and transform his body. Be aware, his transformation might be a bit hulkish in appearance.

When he decides to transform, he'll be able to transform into one or all of the creatures."

"No matter what happens, I'll accept him in any way, shape or form."

"That's good. He'll need that type of support from you."

"How is he doing, old sport?"

"Allie and I were just discussing Eric. Both of us are hoping that he'll come back. One thing that you didn't know is that Victor, Ned and myself imprinted memories and knowledge. It's my opinion that if he does make it, there won't be much training for him. There is also a chance that he will not make it. This is unproven and never done before. His body could reject all of the mixture and basically shut down."

"What do you his chances are?" she asked, tearing up.

"The chances are very high. I've got advance knowledge, he'll be back. The vampire side of him has already visited my thoughts. I'll not spoil the surprise. When I saw him, his body looked very toned. Golden gills appeared on each side of his throat. His eyes were gold and his hair was long and white as the first snow of a winter storm, old sport."

Suddenly, SOMETHING VERY MIRACULOUS occurred in front of Andros, Big Lou and Allie. Eric's clothes vanished from his body. His legs vanished then were replaced with a golden fin. The fin then vanished then his legs changed to that of a werewolf. With long threatening razor sharp claws. A few moments later, the skin of his body turned ghostly white. Typical skin color of a vampire. His short hair then grew long and white as snow flowing well past his shoulders. The height of his body changed from what it was to a hulking six foot seven. Allie sized up his weight, she concluded he now weighed a stout, well-toned, two hundred and ninety pounds. They were all waiting with bated breath for him to open his eyes. A golden aura surrounded his body, then he sat up. When he opened his eyes, they were solid black. Brand new pearly white fangs came from each side of his mouth. He looked around the room then a huge smile came over his face.

"How are you doing old sport?"

"I can truly saw that I have a strong desire for blood. My body also requires some live cattle to feed the hunger of the werewolf in me. My throat feels very dry. My whole body needs to be in water. So, it's a mixed bag of tricks, if you know what I mean?"

"Just as Ned instructed us. You'll need to feed on some deer. That will take care of the vampire side of things. Big Lou will take you to a remote part of our farm. There are some cattle that will feed the werewolf in you. Allie will take you to her diving spot. I've been informed that you've already been there before, old sport."

Eric suddenly moved rapidly around the room. Big Lou provided him with some lose fitting shorts and a shirt. Allie also briefly saw his member, which had doubled in size. This made her smile. Andros noticed that his eyes turned completely black, which told him that Eric needed to do his first feed. Andros took off in a flat sprint toward the east side of his family's farm. Eric smiled then did the same but passed him in only a few seconds. Andros's mouth dropped when he noticed that Eric surpassed him one hundred-fold.

In this distance, Eric saw a royal mount elk feeding on some vegetation. Blood vessels popped in his forehead. Very long, pearly white fangs came out of each side of his mouth. He looked at Andros for approval. He then bowed his head to Eric. Suddenly his legs turned into nothing but a blur. Eric took flight toward the elk. A loud THUD! sounded as he made contact with it. Eric tore into the throat of the elk. It tried to run but Eric had both of its horns in a death grip. Eric could see the blood vessels pumping blood in the animal's body. Another big THUD! sounded as the elk fell then its body convulsed uncontrollably and expired. Using his fangs, he bit deep into the neck then sucked all the blood out of the animal's body. Within seconds, the elk's body turned into ash then blew away with the brisk wind. Eric smiled at Andros as they stood there sizing each other up.

"How do you feel, old sport?"

"My memories showed me that only wildlife is permissible to feed the vampire in me. I feel almost super human."

"That's where you're mistaken, old sport. You're no

longer human, my dear fellow. Remember, you must always use humility. Secrecy is how we've existed for centuries. Can you fly?"

Eric jumped into the air then his body turned into a complete blur. Within micro seconds, Eric landed on front porch. A loud THUD! and SNAP! rang out as he looked at Big Lou and Allie with a smile, a blood soaked face, bloody shirt and shorts. Allie smiled at him. The expression on her race was that of love and thankfulness that he had survived the transformation.

Big Lou gave him some more clothes, which he grabbed moving like superman. He put the new shorts and dark tank top on. It was Big Lou's turn to take him on this first feed as a werewolf. Both of them looked at each other. They both took their clothes off then looked back at Andros and Allie, who both had smiles on their faces. Big Lou, gave off a big HOWL! It sounded like thunder striking down from the heaven. POPPING! CRACKING! rang out as he transformed into a huge alpha wolf. Eric was the next to transform. With his chin high in the air, Eric gave off a big HOWL! as his body transformed into a werewolf. Ironically, he doubled in size compared to Big Lou. They both ran off with their legs turning into a blur until they saw the cattle waiting for their consumption. Big Lou was the first to attack. Using his razor sized claws, he tore the mature cow into shreds, tearing into several pieces. Eric did the same with the next cow. As they both bit into the throat of their cows, blood spurted out on to their faces. Big Lou's and Eric's eyes turned an eerie yellow color. They left nothing but scraps and mayhem. They both ran back to Eric's house. As they jumped toward his deck, they both changed back to human form, naked as the day they were born. Andros and Allie provided them clothes, which they quickly put on to avoid embarrassment. Andros and Big Lou knew that their time was done. They both took off back to Andros family farm. Allie knew it was time for the first dive as a merman for Eric. She wanted it to be relaxed and serene. This would allow him time to adjust his new role in the aquatic world. His powers to hear thoughts and communicate with other living creatures would not come until after his first dive. She thought outside the box then remembered there was still white wine in the refrigerator. Eric moved like the wind then found some wine glasses. She noticed a look of relief on his face. Allie knew that he'd been through a lot with all of the activities with the case. Dealing with that along with making a life changing decision. It was a lot for one person to take. With his new found strength, he easily popped the cork of the wine bottle. He then smelled the cork to make sure the wine was still good.

"It's time for your first dive as a merman. What do you think of that?"

"To be honest, I'm a little excited about it. Also, a little overwhelmed with the things that I must do in order to maintain my existence."

"Look at this way. Before you accepted this change, you'd mentioned for the betterment of mankind. You'd shown the council that a value of human is huge.

Looking around in the room, that comment held a lot of weight in their eyes."

"I guess you're right. I need to have you with me. You being with me, makes me feel complete."

"Aw, thanks Eric Bane. You're even hotter as a hybrid. Your member has doubled in size. It makes me moist even thinking about it."

"Who said you could look at my member?"

"Sorry, just couldn't help it."

With a smile on his face, he grabbed the car keys then they were headed to the Charger. Eric decided to change it up. He threw the car keys to Allie. Her eyes lit up like a Christmas tree. Allie smiled as she turned the car over then revved the engine. Eric grabbed the dash then she peeled out of the driveway.

Fifteen minutes later, they arrived at Bangor Falls National Park. Eric decided to show off a little. In split second, he took off in a flat sprint. His legs were nothing but a blur. Allie smiled but was unable to keep with him. He arrived at the spot then had a big smirk on his face.

"Man, you're a slow poke!"

"Speak for yourself Eric! You damn show off!" she said with a big smile.

The time came for them to dive. Eric was the first to take his clothes off. His arm muscles rippled as he pulled the shirt over his head. Allie did nothing but stare at his ripped chest. She took off her shirt and bra exposing her bodacious breasts. She grabbed them then fondled them in front of him to tease him. He took off his shorts then underwear exposing his eighteen-inch cock. Allie almost slobbered when she saw it. Without hesitation, she took off her shorts then panties. Exposing her moist and hairy crotch to her future husband.

"Hey take a picture, it might last longer. Joke!"

Eric Bane was the first to dive. Allie dove in right after him. Within a couple of seconds, her legs vanished then a fin appeared in their place. She looked over to Eric then her mouth gaped open. His body was spinning in circles with a huge blinding golden light beaming from it. A tattoo of Ned's trident showed up in the middle of his chest. His eyes changed to a golden color. His legs vanished then a yellow fin took their place. They both hit the water at the same time. A big SPLASH! rang out as they went under water. Golden gills both appeared on each side of their throats. He was the first to make it to the bottom. She soon followed him. They both looked at each other than Eric suddenly stopped moving.

It was like he saw something in the distance. Two tridents appeared. One appeared in Eric's hand then the other appeared in Allie's hand. They both saw a diver in scuba gear looking right at them with a fisherman's spear in his hand. He headed right toward them at a rapid speed with the spear. Eric moved with the speed of superman then swam right toward him. He then stood up on his fin and threw the trident at this stranger. The trident stuck in his stomach then Allie swam at him with vengeance on her mind then threw the trident at him. It immediately cut the head off this diver. It quickly rolled to the bottom. Blood gushed from his body. Eric's eyes then turned black as he consumed all of the blood of this stranger. His body then turned into ash underwater then dissolved inside of the water. Eric could hear his thoughts right before Allie killed him. *This is for Katarina and Jody! You blood thirsty freaks of nature.*

Eric's eyes turned back to a golden color. He could hear all kinds of sea life communicating with each other. *It's a good feeling Eric,* Allie said with her mind to him telepathically. *You bet it is. This ability is powerful and must be used with reverence, care and respect,* he answered back to her telepathically. His body then was surrounded by a golden aura. Then it vanished. The same thing happened to Allie. This meant that the dive was complete. They both swam rapidly to the surface then jumped into the air. Their fins vanished then were replaced with legs as they both landed on the same spot they dove from.

"Hey, old sport how you doing?"

This made them both jump three feet in the air. Allie and Eric quickly scurried behind a set of bushes then put their clothes on then gave a glare due to Andros imposing on their privacy.

CHAPTER FIVE
"THE BIGGER THEY ARE, THE HARDER THEY FALL"

Eric WALKED UP TO Andros with the tattoo of the trident still remaining on his chest. Allie grabbed his hand then again glared at him.

"How in the hell did you find our hidden diving spot?"

"Our DNA is linked and please don't forget that. Don't worry, your secret is safe with me. Do you remember that I told you six women and six men were sent to us by the mob out of Chicago?"

"Yeah, what about them?"

"The month that both of you have been gone has been very hard on the Bangor Police Department. Six families that owed the mob have been sexually assaulted, then shot in the right temple as directed. The chief has promoted you both the rank of lieutenant permanently. He's aware the reason you've been gone is one hundred percent justified. He told me to find both of you. His words, please get your asses back to work."

"Six murders, huh? What case does he want us to work on first?"

"The murder of retired police commissioner, Harold Polson, his wife Imelda, and their three boys."

"Was there a vampire mask left by each of the bodies?"

"You bet there was, which to me is very disrespectful of our species."

"Have the bodies been transported to the coroner's office yet?"

"This is the only murder that has not. He wants you, Allie and myself to work the murder scene then try and get some answers for him. The current police commissioner, Mandy Phillips is all over his ass to get this solved. I told him that we would be there in about twenty minutes."

"Let's pile into our Charger then drive to the murder scene. Andros, do you have the address on you?"

"Yes, it's Thirty-two, Forty-four Bangor Maine Terrace Drive. It's fairly close to where our current police chief lives. Oh, by the way, here are your new badges." Andros handed the lieutenant shields to Allie and Eric.

Eric handed Allie the keys then opened the door for her to she get in. He jumped in the passenger seat. Andros jumped in the back seat. Allie turned the car over then peeled out of Bangor Falls National Park and drove to the murder scene as ordered by the chief of police.

Eric and the rest of the crew arrived at the retired police commissioner's house. The junior police recruits had taped off the murder scene. Andros got out first. Eric got out next then opened the door for Allie. They ducked under the tape. Allie and Eric flashed their brand-new lieutenant badges. *I really hate children getting murdered, that really bothers me tremendously,* Eric said to himself. *I would agree with you on that my man,* Allie answered back telepathically.

"I would like to look at the retired police commissioner's body first. It's also my wish that we stay together as a team. This will give us an objective point of observation. You are both aware that I can see the last moments before each death. With my enhanced powers, I might be able to see more. Are you folks OK with working as a team?"

"I'm on board, old sport."

"Me too, Eric."

They walked into the bedroom to find a gruesome mess. The first thing that Andros noticed was high velocity blood spatter on the headboard of the bed. He uncovered the body. The commissioner was shot in the right temple, which linked his murder to the others. The body showed that he was shot in the mouth after the shot to the temple. Allie noticed that there was semen and vaginal fluid all over his groin area, which meant he was forcibly raped. There were also large scratches on the chest of the victim. Andros put on rubber gloves then slightly rolled the victim to his right side. He pointed out that the victim had forcibly been raped in the anal cavity judged by the amount of blood and semen on the outer cheeks of the victim. Eric also noticed several puncture marks in between each toe. *Could the commissioner be a drug user?* he asked himself. He decided to see the last few moments before his death. It would give them more insight as to how the victim lost his life. Andros looked around to make sure no other people would be in eyesight of Eric.

He grasped the commissioner's hand to see if anything would come to light. In a wrinkle of time, Andros, Eric and Allie vanished then reappeared in the room prior to the murder. They hid in the distance to avoid detection.

HAROLD POLSON SAT ON the bed without a care in the world. To his left on the nightstand stood a bag of what appeared to be heroin. He took out a lighter then heated up a spoonful of it. Harold then took a syringe and extracted some of heated substance then put it in between his big toe and the next closest to it. His eyes rolled back then he laid back remaining still as statue. A very chubby older woman walked in wearing nothing but a bra and panties. Harold sat up to talk with his wife.

"You do realize the people that loaned you the money to cover your gambling debts are going to want their money, right?"

"You and I aren't going to be able to cover them. My heroin habit has made me blow through all of my retirement fund. Our mortgage is two months behind. The car payments are also two months behind. We're screwed moneywise, Imelda. Honestly don't what we're going to do."

Without any warning, six women and one man broke

into Harold's house. They went through a sliding glass door, then moved like thieves in the night toward his bedroom. Harold lay on the bed in a drug induced stupor. Imelda sat in a nearby chair reading a woman's magazine. The first woman looked around for jewelry or cash as repayment of the loan to cover his gambling debts. The next five woman walked directly into the bedroom. Imelda had fallen fast asleep in the chair where she sat. Harold, high as kite, got up then got a drink of water to soothe his parched throat. The five women looked like body builders. All with blond hair and breast implants to make up for the steroids they shot up with. In a very quiet approach. One of the women, decided it was time to collect.

"Howdy Harold, do you have my boss's one hundred thousand dollars that he graciously loaned to you?"

"I just need more time. I should have it paid in full within a month."

"You've had six months to repay the boss. It's time to pay the piper. How much cash do you have on hand?"

"There is no cash on hand. What money, I did have, I've spent on heroin."

"You really are a stupid man. The mob loans you the money to cover your gambling debts. Did you really think that the mob is going to let you pay them back on your time? We want the money immediately or you're dead."

"Fuck it, I don't have the money. You can't get blood

out of turnip," he said sarcastically toward the butch women.

The four other women decided to have some fun with him before they slaughtered him and his family. She stripped down exposing her masculine body. Harold got up then tried to run. One of the other women tripped him then threw him on the bed. The rest of them like a bunch of locusts tore all of his clothing off. Another started jerking him off to get him hard. Two other women woke up Imelda to make sure she watched. They taped her eyes open and also tore off all of her clothing. She urinated herself due to extreme fear.

Andros moved in nothing but a blur then ran and got into the purse of the naked woman. Andros quickly scans the driver's license. Yolanda Betner of Chicago Illinois. Eric and Allie did the same thing. They found all of the woman to be sisters and cousins to each other. Eric, Allie and Andros then hid behind a curtain to avoid detection.

Harold's erection would be a good fit the butch woman. She quickly jumped on top of him then rode him like a wild stallion. They forced Imelda to watch her husband getting raped. When she finished the others took their turn until he couldn't hold out anymore. The female held his cock and pointed it towards his face. His cock exploded shooting cum all over his face. Imelda cringed as they forced her to watch. One of them took a big Bowie knife then slit her throat. Harold fought but couldn't overpower the women that were holding him. Blood spatter shot three feet in front of her. Within seconds, she bled out and died. They picked up her bloody body then threw her on her own bed. They placed the vampire mask by her body.

All of them gathered back into Harold's bedroom. Using zip ties, they confined both arms and legs to each of the bed poles. All of the woman pulled their pants down then got on the bed then pissed on his body. One of them also defecated on his belly.

"Yolanda, you've had your fun. Let's end this then get the hell out of here. Hey, Ray Costner, did you kill their boys?"

"Yeah, I did. I shot them all then placed the vampire masks by their heads."

Yolanda pulled out a .38 caliber pistol then shot Harold in the right temple. His body slumped forward. To make sure that he was dead, she opened his mouth then fired another round. Blood and brain matter hit the headboard. She placed the vampire mask by his head then they left like thieves in the night.

THE VISION THEN ENDED when a junior officer tapped Lieutenant Bane on the shoulder saying he had an important call for him. The junior officer handed the cell phone to Lieutenant Bane.

"This is Lieutenant Bane and Lieutenant Phillips. How can we help you?"

"Eric, we found Yolanda, Nancy, Mary, Alex, Jackie Betner staying at the Garden Crest Hotel. I'm aware they were involved with Commissioner Polson's murder. Please drive over there. The SWAT team is already there but hidden. We have jurisdiction in the case. I want you to be the arresting officer. Get them scum bags off the streets. That's not a request, it's an order."

"You got it chief. Andros, Allie and I will drive over there right away."

"That's good news, let's beat feet over there. I also heard the chief wants you to be the arresting officer."

"You and I are the same rank. It doesn't matter with to me."

"Nope, we need to follow the chief's order and have you arrest them. That'll be five of the six women off the streets. It'll also make the current police commissioner, Mandy Phillips happy with the progress of the case."

"Allie, I like the way you drive. Please drive us over there. All of us will assess how these arrests are going to be made."

Eric darted over to the driver's side door then graciously opened the door for Allie. She smiled big then got into the driver's seat. Andros quickly got into the back seat. Eric got into the passenger side front of the Charger. Allie fired it up then peeled out of the driveway of the crime scene and headed to the Garden Crest Hotel. Allie was already familiar as to where the hotel was located into town.

Within ten minutes, they pulled in slowly at the back of the small quaint motel. Over to the left, Andros saw a SWAT van covered in brush. Over to the right, Eric noticed another SWAT van also covered in brush. Eric and Andros decided to use a hidden talent as a vampire. They called it vampire vision. Andros and Eric's pupils turned completely black. Andros got out of the Charger then looked around the east side of the building at ground level. Eric followed him at the roof level. Andros didn't see any snipers at ground level. With a look of anger, Eric spotted two men with sniper rifles, one on the east side roof, the other on west side roof.

"Hey Andros, look up on upper east corner of the roof. There's also another on the upper west side corner."

"Good job, old sport! I bet you those snipers were sent by the mob to protect their employees. How do you want to handle it?"

"Do you remember that sleeper hold that we learned at the academy? That course was a requirement for all consultants and people entering the police force."

"In fact, I do, old sport. I'll take the one on the east corner. You take the one on the west side. Move as fast as you can but be sure nobody sees you. Remember, we have to protect our species with absolute secrecy."

"You got it, buddy."

Moving like a thief in the night, Andros took off in a blur then jumped like a cheetah on top of the roof. Landing ever so softly. The sniper seemed oblivious to Andros standing right behind him. Andros gave a big CHOP! to the left side of the sniper's neck. He immediately went to sleep. He took zip ties then bound his wrists to a huge drain pipe. Then headed back to the

Charger jumping down from the roof at rapid speed then sprinting.

As soon as Andros made it back to the car, Eric took off as if the devil was chasing him. In a matter of three seconds, he stood behind the sniper on the west corner. This sniper also seemed oblivious of Eric's presence. A loud CHOP! came from his hand as he hit the side of his neck. He immediately slumped over and went to sleep. Eric also used zip ties to bind this man to a huge drain pipe. He jumped down like a gazelle then ran with a blur to the Charger.

"There is no clear and present danger to the SWAT team. These arrests should go off without a problem."

"I would agree, old sport."

Andros, Allie pulled out their pistols then placed their Lieutenant badges on their belts. Andros did the same. They walked over to the SWAT van on the right then noticed they had video surveillance in the room that the Betner Group decided to hide in. *They decided to stay all in the same room. This arrest is going to be cinch,* Eric thought to himself. Andros, Allie and Eric looked at each other at the same time. It was time to have a meeting to discuss the strategy for the arrest.

"This arrest is going to be a cinch. There are five of them. We can't just go in there guns a blazing. We need to plan that will not cause harm or loss of life."

"Maybe, we don't use guns at all. We could do one of two things. The SWAT team could just shoot tear gas or sleeping gas inside the room. Another idea might be to use blow darts then put them to sleep one by one. We could use some smelling salts to wake them up. What do you think, Andros?"

"I'm thinking that we should use tear gas in the room. It'll force them out then we could arrest them. Using sleeping gas or darts may be too brutal in the eyes of a judge. We got to make sure the case is air tight. Just so you know, we may have got rid of the threat of the mob for the moment. But they're going to have their lawyers use everything possible to get their clients off, old sport."

"That approach sounds like a good one. Andros is right, dealing with mob can be a little bit complicated. Let's make it happen. The chief is on our butts to get these arrests done."

Lieutenant Bane instructed the SWAT team to shoot some tear gas inside of the room. Crews from both sets of SWAT team members were moving slowly to room 234 of the Garden Crest Hotel. Yolanda and the rest of the girls were oblivious to the SWAT team approaching. Allie watched in the window. Yolanda stood at a table using a razor to cut lines of cocaine for them to enjoy. Hard rock punk music drowned out any outside sounds, which masked the approach the team.

Using his enhanced vision, Andros saw to the right of Yolanda there stood a pile of the vampire masks they were using in the murders. This angered Andros as he continued to watch. Allie closed her eyes to listen to their thoughts. They appeared to be planning the next kill, which would be directed toward the current mayor of Bangor Maine, Tony Shuto. Andros also saw a small pile of automatic assault rifles. *We could add this to the battery of charges, when we arrest them,* Andros thought as he continued to watch. Two of the team leaders loaded tear gas grenades in their specially designed assault rifles. They were just waiting for the green light from Eric. There were two windows in the room. One on the east side and other window on the west side. Eric gestured them with a big thumbs up. Andros and Eric, with their enhanced hearing heard each sniper shoot the grenade. A big WHISP! came in the air as the grenade came close to contact with the window, which would break easily due to the speed and velocity of the grenade. A big CRASH! rang out in each of the windows as they shattered due to the impact of the grenades. The grenades landed strategically in front and behind of Yolanda Betner. Tear gas clouded the room as all of the Betner group began to cough and almost gasp because they couldn't breathe. They ran out of the motel room with their hands up. SWAT members swarmed them like a bunch of locusts. They immediately made all of them get on their knees. Each of the woman were zip tied with their hands behind their back. Eric, Andros and Allie approached them walking briskly until they were in front of Yolanda Betner.

"Yolanda, Nancy, Mary, Alex, Jackie Betner, you are under arrest for the rape and murder of Commissioner Harold Polson. Also, for the murders of Imelda Polson and the three murders of the minor male children. You are also under arrest for possession of cocaine and illegal assault weapons. You have the right to remain silent, if you give up that right all of what you say will be

held against you in a court. You have the right to an attorney. If you can't afford an attorney, the City of Bangor Maine will appoint you one at low cost. Do you understand these rights as I've disclosed them to you?" Lieutenant Bane asked with his eyes glued on Yolanda Betner.

"What is your name sir?"

"My name is Lieutenant Bane, this is Lieutenant Phillips and special consultant to the Bangor Maine Police Department, Andros Surkacksi. Do you understand your rights? Do you wish to give a statement at this time?"

"All of us understand our rights. We'll be out before the ink is dry on any charges that you file against us. No, we don't wish to give a statement at this time."

"Take these pieces of human trash to jail!"

The SWAT team followed Eric's orders to the letter. They took all of the Betner group then placed them in a van then sped off out of the motel parking lot. Allie looked at Eric with adoring eyes. This was the first time she saw him arrest anybody. *Wow! What a big stud!* she thought. *Why thank you!* he answered back telepathically with a big naughty smile on his face.

"Please get down!" Andros yelled as he jumped to the ground for safety.

Just as the SWAT vans pulled off the main road then stopped suddenly. Allie and Eric jumped to the ground. With their enhanced hearing, all of them put an expression of fear on their faces. A big WHISP! rang out as two rockets headed right for the van. Eric heard them going in rapid circles as they got closer to the SWAT vans. Their heartbeats increased and their breathing lessened as they finally made contact with the van. A hung BANG! rang out as the van exploded then turned on its side engulfed in flames. Allie and Eric felt saddened as they heard the cries of their soon to be fallen comrades.

"Holy Shit! That's what we get for dealing with the mob. The Betner group to the mob just turned into a loose end. These people mean business. They are ruthless in their pursuit of fulfilling their orders of the big mob bosses in Chicago. Oh well, we've done our due diligence."

The Bangor Maine Fire Department came out and put of the fire. There were no survivors, which pissed off Allie, Andros and Eric. Their mouths gaped open in horror of what they just witnessed. Eric saw something out of the corner of his eye. There was a man running on foot. Using his enhanced vision, he saw Ray Costner running with a black bag in his hands. Both Andros and Eric took off like greased lightning towards him. They tackled him then the black bag went flying out of his hands three yards from where he landed. Andros quickly got him to his knees then zip tied his hands behind his back. Both Andros and Eric recognized him from the vision they had before. Allie caught up to them then smiled because they would have the ability to arrest someone for the senseless murder of the Polson family.

"*Ray Costner, you are under arrest for the rape and murder of Commissioner Harold Polson. Also, for the murders of Imelda Polson and the three murders of the minor male children. You are also under arrest for possession of cocaine and illegal assault weapons. Lastly, your also under arrest for all of the people you just killed in that SWAT vans. You have the right to remain silent, if you give up that right all of what you say will be held against you in a court. You have the right to an attorney. If you can't afford an attorney, the City of Bangor Maine will appoint you one at low cost. Do you understand these rights as I've disclosed them to you?"*

"I was just getting rid of some loose ends for my bosses. Yes, I understand my rights. Just as Yolanda told you, I'll be out before the ink is dry on your paperwork. I don't wish to give you any statement at this time."

The team captain walked over then took custody of Ray Costner. They also took custody of the black bag containing the portable launcher. They placed him in an unmarked vehicle then sped off toward the jail with their prisoner. Andros and Eric were on the alert as they watched the other SWAT van drive off. They looked left then right to make sure there were no more surprises. Within ten minutes, the SWAT van made it to the jail with Ray Costner in tow.

"Phew! That was a close one. At least we're able to get an arrest done properly. Allie, you and I would never hear the end of it from the chief," he said with a big sigh of relief on his face."

"Good Job, old sport. You saw Ray Costner before I did. That means your powers as a hybrid far exceed mine. I'm extremely proud of you, my brother!"

"No need to give me praise. I was just doing my job. Part of the training memories they placed inside of me is to use my gifts with prudence and care. Also, not to use them for personal gain. Humility is going to be my approach in all of this."

"Take compliments when they come your way. I do understand your approach. It's one of a seasoned and wise vampire. Listen, my father and I had a chance to talk about what happened to you and Allie on your first dive. Somebody knows your secrets, which put you at extreme risk. My father had a thousand gallons of ocean water flown in from the seas of Greece. They've placed the huge tank in the barn. It's under heavy guard. I'm aware that you and Allie need to dive soon to recharge your batteries. Will you accept my father's gesture of good will toward you?"

"That would be completely up to the love of my life. It's my duty to make sure that she is safe and out of harm's way."

"When I dive, it's a very sacred and private thing. That's why I chose the spot that I did. You're right Andros, I guess Eric and I can accept your father's gesture of good will. Only if Eric is OK with it," she said with a look of approval from Eric.

"If Allie is OK with it, then so am I."

"My father took the liberty of contacting Ned. He's already blessed the water for your use. He provided us with some undersea life to heighten the experience. Big Lou also told me that he's very proud of how you're carefully using your powers as a hybrid. Victor is also very happy as to how you're using them."

"Be sure to pass on my thanks. I do have to admit, I'm feeling very weak. The blood pumping in Allie's veins is looking like a sirloin steak to me. The vampire in me is very hungry right now. I vowed to all of who attended the meeting never to take a human or any other creature without expressed permission from the council."

"Don't fret, old sport. Let's drive to our family farm. Due to the success of our case, I have a forty-five-year-old snifter of cognac to share with you and Allie."

"What you about you Allie. Are you hungry and ready to enjoy some cognac with Andros and his family?"

"Yes, but my love needs to feed. I'm very concerned about you, my love. Plus, you and I will need to dive soon. Andros did you want to share your cognac before or after we take care of our current needs?"

"Of course, after. I can see his eyes are turning completely black, which means that he's dangerous to be around until he feeds."

"I've also been informed they have trapped a mountain lion for you to consume on our land. Big Lou also has two head of cattle for you to feed the werewolf in you."

"My love, it's time to drive to the Andros's family farm if you're in agreement. Also, you've not eaten any human food for a very long time. I'm a little worried about you Allie."

"My father also thought of that. They have a big prime rib dinner ordered from The Anchor Bay Steak and Lobster House. Just for you. The owner also included a vintage bottle of nineteen seventy-eight bottle of wine for you."

"Victor has proved to be a very thoughtful and caring member of our family. Let's drive up there then take care of business."

They all walked briskly to the Charger. Eric threw the keys to Allie. He graciously opened the door for her. She got in and turned the Charger over then listened to the engine purr like kitten. Eric got into the passenger side then Andros got in the back. Allie peeled rubber then headed to the Surkacksi Farm. Eric snickered as he watched Andros's white knuckles on the head rest in front of them. A fear of getting into a wreck plagued his face. Fifteen minutes later, they made to the farm. Victor greeted them as Allie parked the Charger.

He took Allie by the hand then went into the family house then into the dining room. Steam rolled off the huge piece of prime ribs as its scent wafted its way back to Allie's nose. Two house servants both took her by the arm and had her sit as they served her. There stood a big garden salad with succulent cherry tomatoes with butter lettuce and red onions with blue cheese dressing. There was a huge goblet of au jus to pour all over her prime rib if she chose to do so. Victor popped the cork to the wine then sniffed it. This was to make sure it was suitable for Allie to enjoy. He poured her a glass of wine for her then for himself. Allie felt ravenous and wasted no time in enjoying the meal fit for a member of the royal family.

Meanwhile back with Andros and Eric five miles into a tree grove thick of trees…

ERIC AND ANDROS WATCHED as one of the servants of the home freed the mountain lion. Big Lou was in the eastern part of the farm close by tending to the two head of cattle waiting for Eric to feed on them. Eric watched as the mountain lion raced toward the head of cattle by. *I'm so hungry. I haven't eaten in days. Those cows look very yummy for me,* the mountain lion thought.

Eric could hear the thoughts of the mountain lion. He ripped off the shirt he was wearing. His eyes turned completely black and the blood vessels popped in his forehead. Andros also tore his shirt off and looked the same way that Eric did. They looked at each other then took off in a blur toward the mountain lion. The lion saw Eric, which made him stop in his tracks. They both lunged at each other. When Eric and the mountain lion hit each other in the air, a big THUD! rang out as Eric savagely bit into the lion's throat as they both hit the ground. Andros jumped in then bit on the opposite side of Eric. Blood shot into Eric's mouth, which he drank like he hadn't eaten in days. Andros also sucked the blood hungrily and savagely. The lion shook and pawed at both of them. Eric continuously and savagely bit further into the lion's neck. The lion convulsed then a big GROWL! rang out from his mouth. Moments later, the mountain lion succumbed to Eric and Andros feeding on it. Within seconds, due to the drinking of all of its blood the mountain lion disincarnated into dust, which blew away in a brisk wind.

Andros sped off back to the farm to allow Eric some privacy. A very big HOWL! rang out from Eric's lips as a big snout came from his face. His arms and legs were replaced with paws that were razor sharp. Fangs came out of his mouth as the reminder of his clothes tore off. The pupils in his eyes turned into the color of blood. Big Lou also transformed into a werewolf. He looked a bit fearful of Eric, who dwarfed the already huge size of Big Lou. They both savagely ran after the two head of cattle. Eric dove then tore out the throat of his animal. With his paws he tore the belly open then savagely ate all of the organs and then drank all of its blood. In a fraction of second, the animal disincarnated into dust, which blew away in the wind. Big Lou did the same and his animal also disincarnated into dust that also blew away in the wind. Moments later, Big Lou and Eric then transformed back into their human form. They quickly jumped into a nearby reservoir to wash all the blood and entrails off their bodies.

Allie watched her man get out of the reservoir and saw his big member, which immediately made her moist. Victor and she brought big robes for both of them. Eric looked like he had satisfied two of three. She knew he was ready to take a dive in the big tank to recharge the merman inside of him. Andros and Victor had an expression of pride on their faces as they led Eric and Allie to the barn. There was a ten-foot ladder they both had to climb to jump into the tank of ocean water.

Victor and Andros left to give them privacy to do their dive.

THEY BOTH MADE IT to the top of the ladder. They looked at each other with adoring eyes. Allie took off her shirt and bra letting her bodacious and yummy tits fall out freely. She then took off her pants and panties exposing her very hairy bush to Eric. His already big member swelled into a gigantic erection. This made Allie lick her lips then smile seductively at him as she jumped. Eric then followed in right behind her. The thousand-gallon tank was more than enough for them to regenerate their aquatic powers. Eric's body spun in circles as a golden ray surrounded it as he swam then sat on the surface of the tank. The trident tattoo shined brightly as he lay on the surface. His eyes turned into a bright, shiny golden color. Their legs were quickly replaced with fins but were a bit late because they hadn't dived for a long time. Allie's body shined a golden color as she recharged her aquatic batteries. The golden gills on each side of their throats shined brightly.

"Even though, we haven't been made love yet, I need to tell you that I love you Eric with all of my heart, mind and soul."

"I've loved you since the first time I laid eyes on you at my favorite spot that I use to think about my cases. I love you too, with all my heart, mind and soul."

"I would like to have an opportunity to propose to you when the time is right. In our culture, it's customary that the mermaid proposed to the merman. It's not the other way around, so please respect our culture and traditions."

"I have no problem with our culture. Please make it soon. In my family, it's taboo to have sex outside of marriage. I've been wanting to ravage your body since I first laid eyes on you."

The diving ritual completed, they both jumped from the surface of the tank. They bypassed the ladder then headed to the floor of the barn. Eric landed first. His feet gently landed as he then caught Allie in his arms. Ned, Victor, Andros and Big Lou were there with robes and towel.

"My fine boy, you've evolved into an exceptional merman. You've embraced your role and under our guidelines."

"I can speak for the vampire race. Eric, you've evolved into an exceptional vampire. You respected our wishes to only feed on wildlife. Never feed on a human and respect them and keep them safe and free of any harm," Victor said as he patted Eric on the back.

"I can speak for the werewolf race. Eric, you've evolved into an exceptional werewolf. In fact, you dwarf me in size. In fact, you kind of scare the shit out of me with your gigantic size. I guess it's the mixture of three creatures in your body. Hats off to you, my good fellow."

"Thank you for all of your compliments. However, I choose to remain humble and contrite in my role. I've embraced all of your races with grace and finesse. Thanks again my dear friends and family."

"My fine mermaid daughter, have you proposed to him yet?"

"Nope not yet but plan too very shortly."

"You'd better do it soon. I'm looking forward to embracing my role as Grand Merman to my grandchildren."

"Stop it Dad, you're embarrassing me," she said as her cheeks flushed in front of her future husband.

"I have some good news and some bad news for all of you," one of the servants said to them.

"Our estate just got a call from your police chief, Harry Montel. He's informed me that Mayor Tony Shuto has received death threats from the mob. He's assigned you and Lieutenant Phillips as part of the protective detail personally for the mayor. His exact words were this is not a request, it's an order."

"I guess our cognac is going to have to wait."

ERIC, ANDROS AND ALLIE found suitable business attire then headed to the Charger to drive to the mayor's home to become part of the protection detail. Allie already had the keys so she jumped into the driver's seat. Eric closed her door then got into the passenger seat. Andros had a regretful look in eyes as he got into the back seat of what he called the Death Charger. She sped off but then looked at Eric with love and admiration.

"Andros what's the address for Mayor Shuto's home?"

"Let's see the servant told me that the chief provided as part of the message. The address is Twenty-two, Twenty-two Bangor Falls Road. It's pretty close to your old diving spot Allie."

"How close is his house in relation to the park? I ask you that because I don't recall seeing a home in the park."

"Right before you get to the entrance of the park, there's a dirt road that leads to his home."

"Now I remember the road. I guessed that dirt road didn't lead anywhere."

"You learn something new every day, huh," Eric said with a small smirk on his face.

Eric could see the look of anticipation on Allie's face. She appeared fearless but also cautious at the same time as she drove to the mayor's private residence. Andros also looked a little fearful. *I wonder if we'll be successful with the mayor. So far, this case is pretty complex and needs to be handled with finesse,* Eric said to himself as they entered the driveway of the mayor's house.

They ran into an array of unmarked police cars. A checkpoint created to protect the mayor and his family. Eric, Allie and Andros flashed their badges then they pulled into the driveway. The house itself looked like something built in the Victorian era. Late nineteenth century designed with outdoor crown moldings around the window. Andros was the first to get out of the Charger. He looked around then walked up to the porch of the light brown house. Eric got out then opened the door for Allie. They both walked right up behind Andros. A big man walked up to the door then opened it with a welcoming smile. Mayor Tony Shuto shook everyone's hands. With his burly six-foot three frame and around four hundred pounds, the mayor himself appeared to be very welcoming and humble to anyone coming to his home. His wife Nancy walked toward them looked quite rotund. She stood around five foot two and a very rotund four hundred pounds. The mayor poured everyone a cup of coffee.

"Good morning your honor. My team and I were informed from the chief that there have been some death threats towards your family. We've just joined your security detail. All of us will do our best to protect you and your family."

"Please call me Tony even though I do appreciate the respect you show to me. The threats started with my two girls at school. One of them is fourteen years old and the other is seventeen. They both checked their lockers at school. When they opened their locker, they each found a vampire mask and a note. The note said, you and your family are next! Signed by the Chicago Mob. When I saw and heard about this, I called your chief. He told me the same masks were showing up at murder scenes. When security found out about it, they instantly pulled my two daughters out of school. My wife, who works for the fire department was also pulled. All of them are here in protective custody. From what the chief told me, these guys from the mob are very brutal. My family means the world to me. If anything happens to me or my family."

"I show no disrespect toward you and your family, but a question needs to be asked in order to get a clear understanding as to why they are threatening your family."

"Lieutenant Bane and Lieutenant Phillips, please ask me anything you want to."

"Have anyone loaned you or any of your staff money from a office based out of Chicago?"

"Yeah why, I had a campaign contribution to my role as mayor. Our staff didn't take it as a loan but as a donation."

"Who loaned you the money?"

"Trent Lechesky is who gave the money to my campaign for mayor."

"He is the son of Alex Lechesky, a big member of a brutal mafia group."

"What was the amount they paid you?" Allie asked with a worried look on her face.

"You wouldn't believe me if I told you."

"If we are to protect you, you'll need to be transparent one hundred percent to us."

"The information that I'm about to disclose to you is private and confidential."

"You bet it is sir, how much?"

"Trent sent a check to my office for five million dollars. In fact, all of it was used to get me elected as mayor."

"The money you spent is blood money. The mafia is

coming to either get the money from you or kill you and every member of your family. In their eyes, the money sent to you has two things in common. One is political favors and if they don't get that from you, they want to collect the money from you by any means necessary. If they can't recoup the money, you and your family will pay with your lives."

"What needs to be done here? How can I protect my family?"

"That's a question that I can't answer as far as the money is concerned. The feds are going to have to help you with that. As far as your family, they are in extreme danger. We just made an arrest in the Commissioner Polson matter. This one might be beyond our control. The Lechesky family has a big reach in this town. They are ruthless, brutal and have no regard for human life."

"Andros, what do you think we should do to handle this?"

"Old sport, judging by what I've just heard, we should protect the mayor and his family the best way we can. If he agrees to testify against them, he'll be signing his own death warrant. He may have to go into the witness protection program with the feds."

Eric and Andros with their enhanced hearing discovered something was coming. A loud SREECH! of car brakes came to their ears. Andros ran outside noticed in the background four vans pulling up to the check point. A man pointed a semi-automatic weapon out of the window then opened fire on three of the members of the police department. Shooting them dead on the spot. The look of extreme fear came over Mayor Shuto and his wife. Beads of sweat rolled down his brow as he and his wife hid behind Eric and Andros inside of their home. *What in the hell should we do here?* Eric asked himself. Then a light bulb went off in his head. He quickly called the chief then asked him to have the SWAT team drive in and also fly in with a helicopter. His hands shook as he explained to the chief all of what's going on. He informed him that the calvary was on their way. Including the support of the feds. With his hands still shaking, he hung up the phone.

"The chief said to hold out, the calvary is on its way including the feds. He told we just need to protect Mayor Shuto at all costs."

"This is going to make quite a shit storm. My obligation to protect and serve. The mayor, his wife and children need to go into their bedroom then lock the door. No one is to enter that room unless the immediate threat to their lives has subsided," Allie said as she grabbed Nancy's hand then led her to the bedroom.

"Mayor Shuto, please follow them into your bedroom. Please don't come out until you've heard from us."

Tony Shuto took his girls then walked swiftly into their bedroom. The expression on his face was one of deep regret.

"Eric and Allie, get down!"

A big WHIRLING! sound came from the distance. A rocket made its way toward the front window. Allie came back in then hit the floor to avoid harm. Andros did the same but Eric stood there then clapped his hands together. Suddenly, a golden aura surrounded the whole room. As soon as the rocket came in, Eric grabbed it then turned around then pointed up toward the sky.

A loud WHISSHNG! sound came from it as Eric directed it out to the sky. There was a nearby pile of rocks in the distance. The rocket went up to the sky then headed right for the pile of rocks. A loud BANG! came from the pile of rocks. It exploded upon contact. Eric then fell to his knees with a big sigh of relief. By that time, Andros and Allie heard five helicopters approaching with two SWAT vans speeding to get behind them. Before Eric got up the loud sounds of automatic weapons rang out. Twenty of the mobsters sent to kill the Shuto family dropped like dominoes. The helicopters ordered the SWAT team to move away. They shot their own rockets then annihilated all of the mobsters. Dead bodies littered the driveway and yard of the mayor. Within seconds, federal agents swarmed the Shuto household and took immediate custody of the mayor, his wife and the two children then swiftly put them in a helicopter and flew off as if the devil was chasing their tails. Allie got up with her mouth gaping open. Andros got up looking very pale. They all stood there trying to calm their nerves.

"You're next to explain what the hell just happened Eric."

"You showed the power of a god. How in the hell did you pull it off, old sport? We could have gotten seriously injured or killed if you wouldn't have done that," he said as he patted Eric on the shoulder.

"Ned appeared in my thoughts then guided me to do it to save lives. The trident on my chest burned like it was one fire when I made contact with the rocket. He is the one that helped me save all of your lives."

"I've just been informed the feds are going to clean all of this up. Let's get the hell out of this hell and mayhem. This made me hungry for a burger. What about you Eric?"

"You know Allie, a big hamburger with all the fixings sounds good."

"I concur, old sport."

Allie walked with them to the Charger. Eric opened the door the her then she got in. Andros got in with a dreadful look. Eric got in with a huge expression on satisfaction on his face. She turned the car over then listened to it purr. She drove to Ed's burgers with a look of phew on her face. As they pulled, Eric asked her to park for a moment before they went in.

"Listen, we have Lori Betner left to arrest and that will be all of the women sent by the mob. We arrested Ray Costner, which leaves five more guys to capture to at least slow the mob down. The question is, how are we going to get them? Unless we have another murder, we have no way of catching them or preventing them from killing anymore of our citizens. Any suggestions from the two of you?"

Meanwhile at the residence of Clyde Smith, sheriff of the Bangor Maine Sheriff's Department...

CLYDE SMITH, AN OBESE man of four hundred pounds and around six feet tall, sat at his desk chain smoking cigarettes like they were going out of style. He looked at his balding red hair and huge beard in a mirror for a fraction of a second to check for pimples. A loud DING! rang out from his laptop. He looked at the screen then noticed an email from Trent Lechesky. His mouth gaped open when he read the contents of email. *Shit due to the loan to cover my gambling debts that he loaned has put me into some hot water. What the hell am I going to do. They want payment in full?* Clyde thought to himself as he lit up another smoke. As he shut the lid to his laptop. *An ice-cold beer sounds good,* he thought to himself as he walked up to the refrigerator to grab one. Just as he reached into the refrigerator for the beer, he had the feelings somebody was in his kitchen with him.

A very tall man standing six feet seven in height and around two hundred and seventy-five pounds stood there looking at him. With his long blond hair and very blue eyes, he looked a little miffed at Clyde. He looked to be a man of Swedish descent. As his heartbeat increased beads of sweet rolled down his cheeks.

"Clyde Smith, you've been a very bad boy. Trent covered all of your one hundred thousand dollars in poker debts. You were quick to receive the money but slow to pay my boss back his money. Why is that happening my good fellow?" he asked with a Swedish accent.

"Before I go any further, I want to know who is the hell I'm talking to."

"My name Evan Solcareh. You need to cough up the money as right now sir, otherwise I'm going to put a world of hurt on you."

"I can't give what I don't have."

Evan pulled out a set of brass knuckles then placed them on his right hand. The sheriff went to grab a knife to protect himself. Before he knew it, Evan hit him very hard in the right rib cage. POPPING and CRACKING! rang out from Clyde's body as he doubled over. He tried to stand up straight. Evan swung a right-handed punch to the side of the temple. Clyde fell on his back to the ground. He then punched Clyde's face with several strikes to each of his cheeks. To add insult to injury, Evan broke his nose. Blood spurted out over his clean police uniform. He then placed his foot right on the throat.

"You have twenty-four hours to pay up. Otherwise, they'll be taking you out of here in a box. Have I made myself clear, my good fellow?"

"Young man, you're crystal clear, you fucking asshole!"

Evan smirked then strutted out of the sheriff's house at 5607 Fox Trot Lane. The sheriff stumbled to his home phone then called himself an ambulance. Being an old bachelor, he couldn't rely on anybody else.

Meanwhile an hour later at Ed's Burgers with Allie, Eric and Andros...

ERIC SMIRKED AS HE watched Allie take a big bite out of her greasy burger. Andros giggled as grease ran down her arm. Both them didn't eat food anymore as they drank blood to maintain their existence. His cell rang as he took a big gulp of grape soda.

"Lieutenant Bane, can I help you?"

"Eric, this is Harry. Sheriff Clyde Smith just got the crap beat out of him at this home. Our other guys could've handled it. That is not the reason I called you. He gave the name of Evan Solcareh. Clyde described him as six feet seven in height and around two hundred and seventy-five pounds. He told me that he has long blond hair with blue eyes. Evan Solcareh is one the names flagged for being one of the six men sent to us by the mob. I want to you get your butts over to the hospital then talk with sheriff."

"Let me guess he got a loan from Trent Lechesky and his motley crew."

"You'd be right, the sheriff admitted to me that he had over one hundred thousand dollars in poker or gambling debts."

"You got it, boss. We'll head over to Bangor Memorial Hospital and talk with Clyde."

"I want this Evan Solcareh behind bars as soon as soon as you can."

"My crew and I will do our best."

CHAPTER SIX
"BROKEN IN TWO"

"THE BOSS JUST TOLD me that Sheriff Clyde Smith just got the crap beat of him for gambling debts paid by the one, the only, Trent Lechesky. He wants us to visit him in at Bangor Memorial. Harry said that he's six feet seven in height and around two hundred and seventy-five pounds with blond hair and blue eyes. His also said the gentleman's name is Evan Solcareh. He also told me that guy is of Swedish descent."

"This guy sounds like he's the size of Viking, old sport."

"That's what I thought too. We need to drive to Bangor Memorial right now. That's if you guys are up to it."

"There is no rest for the wicked. I think that Andros and I are up it."

Eric paid Allie's hamburger with his debit card. They walked out and all of them got into the Charger. Allie, of course, got in the driver's seat. This put a big smile on her face because it showed that he trusted her. She fired up the Charger then peeled out of Ed's Burgers parking lot. Eric smiled as Andros had a death grip on the head rest from the backseat.

Within fifteen minutes, they made it to Bangor Memorial. They walked into the hospital then went to the front desk. They flashed their badges then took the elevator up the second floor. The charge nurse said that

Clyde Smith was housed in room 201. A couple of minutes later, they made it to his room. Allie's mouth gaped open on how bad the sheriff looked. His face looked swollen and his nose had a metal piece taped to hold it into place. Andros checked and Clyde seemed to be awake and ready to talk with them.

"Hey sheriff, it looks like you got the crap beat of you buddy. Your department is separate from ours. I almost never see you or any of your deputies."

"I would agree, when you were younger, you always wanted to ride in my cop car. This is my own damn fault. I'm an old cantankerous bachelor. I play a lot of poker both online and with friends. I racked up a big gambling debt, which Trent Lechesky covered. The amount of money I owe him is one hundred thousand dollars. I got an email from him demanding to get paid. Then he sends this asshole to collect from me. He beat the crap out of me then told me he wanted his boss's money within twenty-four hours. I think that he's going to kill me. I would say that I'm in clear and present danger."

"Why isn't there a protective detail assigned to you?"

"The sheriff's department doesn't have much of a budget. This is due to the county reducing our budget. I'm hoping that Harry and his force can provide me one."

"Andros, give the boss a call while Clyde and I chat. I'm sure he'll be able to help him. We always take care of our own."

"No problem, old sport. I'll go outside then make the call."

Andros and Allie left the room to give Eric and the sheriff some privacy. As she left, her eyes were adoring looking at him.

"Clyde, is there a safe house where we could take you?"

"No, we lost the funding. I really have no place to go, Eric."

"You could stay at my house. The chief hired a bunch of new police officers fresh out of the academy. I'm sure he'll agree to protect you. What else can you tell me about Trent Lechesky?"

"He's the type of guy that's very nice and cordial. When you turn your back that man would stab you just as soon look at you."

"How did you get in contact with him?"

"His dad Alex is a family friend. I really didn't know much about them but just by acquaintance."

"Alex Lechesky is a member of the Chicago Mafia. From what I can understand, he's a high-ranking member of it. His son helps him launder money and also serves as a loan officer or collector of people that won't pay him back. Sheriff, your life is important to not only me but our police department. You were just naïve about the Lechesky family. Not to show any disrespect towards you. You're a very foolish man. You know you could've come to me for help. I've known you since I was a teenager."

"I already know. I hope you can help me get out of this shit storm of trouble."

"My department and I will do our best. Did you hear that I just got promoted to lieutenant?"

"Yeah, I heard about that and forgot to come and see you to congratulate you. Congrats my boy."

As soon as Eric turned to look at the door. a huge man walked in wearing an orderly uniform. He looked to be six feet seven in height and around two hundred and seventy-five pounds with blond hair and blue eyes. A look of horror came over Clyde's face as Evan Solcareh walked closer to his bed. Two other men walked in right behind him. Blood vessels popped out of Eric's forehead as he walked right up to Clyde's bed.

"Mr. Solcareh, you do realize that you'll never make it out of the hospital. Sheriff Clyde Smith isn't going anywhere with you or any other of your associates."

"My good fellow, I'm an honorable man but also have to do my job. Clyde Smith, do you have my boss's money?"

"I'll never pay you. Lieutenant Bane has informed me who you work for and what your organization represents. Get the hell out of my room!"

Suddenly, everybody stood still as statues in the room including Eric. He was able to move his eyeballs to his watch then noticed time had stopped.

"By the power of Oden, I call upon you the powers of old," Evan said as his body transformed.

An eerie gold light surrounded his body. A helmet with ivory horns on each side of it appeared on his head. His eyes turned into a blinding white color. His size already huge transformed into a man of seven foot one and over five hundred pounds. His clothes were removed then replaced with pelts of furs from animals of old. His shoes were replaced with sandals with leather straps going half way up his leg. A double-sided ax showed up in his hand, razor sharp as it glistened in the well-lit room. Two of the men behind him walked up to the hospital bed then grabbed up the sheriff. He glared at Eric as he walked out of the room.

Everything and everyone couldn't move. The only ones able to move were Evan and his associates. The trident shined brightly inside of Eric's chest. *Shit! I can't move and help the sheriff,* Eric thought to himself as he tried to reach Andros and Allie. The only thing working in Eric's favor was that he could hear. A loud SCREECH! came out in the parking lot as Evan and his henchmen drove off in a van with the sheriff.

A freakish moment later, time restarted and all things were able to move in. Andros knocked the door off its hinges as he ran into the room. Allie had a very pissed off look on her face as she ran in right behind him.

"What the hell just happened? I couldn't move and time had stopped judging by the clock on the wall. I was able to get ahold of the boss. He agreed to setup a security detail for the sheriff, old sport."

"Somebody with unearthly and almost godlike powers made this happen. I too couldn't move.

Nothing in the world has had the ability to stop me. Eric what did you see? Where in the hell is Sheriff Clyde Smith?"

"Evan Solcareh stopped time. He called upon the Viking god Oden. He transformed into a huge Viking creature. The sheriff is gone. Evan and his group took him then took off in a van. I heard the screech of loud car brakes in the outside parking lot of the hospital. We are dealing with a big unknown. Are either of you familiar with Viking mythology?"

"No, old sport. I've never really had the opportunity to study it or deal with it."

"We're up against another hurdle. Until we can learn to defend ourselves against these dark arts, we are going to be defenseless. There's no way to tell where they took the sheriff. Even though he's chain smoking fool, he was my father's closest friend. His department is separate from ours but he's still one of our own. I'm just wondering how we're going to proceed from here."

"There is one thing that needs to be pointed out. Evan has to stay in our realm in order to communicate with his boss in Chicago. This tells me that he's still here in Bangor."

"I hope the hell you're right Allie. The only question is what can we do to defend ourselves against these dark arts?"

"That's a question that I can answer," the chief said as he snuck up behind Eric.

"Holy shit boss, you scared the hell out of me. How

much do you know of what happened?"

"Enough to know that you're dealing with a dark art that I'm familiar with."

HARRY MONTEL ASKED EVERYONE to sit down in the room. Eric, Allie and Andros wanted to know how much he knew of the case. Also, they wondered how much he knew about their true nature. Did he know that Andros existed as a vampire, Allie existed as a mermaid and Eric was a mixture of all three including having traits of werewolf?

Harry walked up to the middle of the group. With his very smooth shaved head and well-trimmed goatee, he placed his hands on his lap. All of them felt a sense of fear and dread. At an age of fifty-nine years old and his hulking height of six-foot four frame with a very well-toned and chiseled weight of two hundred and five pounds, the chief could be a little intimidating at times. Harry's eyes as dark as two lumps of coal also showed wisdom and experience. Eric felt a little nervous as he waited for the chief to start speaking.

"I'm getting the vibe from all of you folks that you want to know much I know of what went on and also the true nature or existence of all of you. I've tried to remain hands off to most of you but this case and what's happened in your lives is bigger that any of us. I was able to tap into Evan's memory for a small wrinkle of time. He is a direct descendant from some of the most feared, brutal and devoted followers of Oden in Viking history. Clyde Smith is still in Bangor. Evan is forbidden to take him into the very ancient realm. I know that because I have a Masters in the study of their culture, religion, and the limitations of their powers. One thing that I can tell you. What Evan did is forbidden in the worship of Oden. He may be stripped of some of his powers. We are going to have to track them down here in Bangor. There is a totem or walking stick that I have in the back of my car trunk that blocks him from using his powers. The walking stick also bars him from leaving our realm. I'm now taking command of this case. All of us are going to be working together at least until we get Sheriff Clyde Smith safe and back with us.

"I don't know if you know this. The city of Bangor Maine, under its charter has the legal authority to dissolve the sheriff's department. I'm in charge of blending Clyde's department with our own. He'll still be the sheriff until his term is up. The police commissioner is going to promote him to the rank of captain after that takes place. This is due to lack of funding for his dissolving department. He and I will share in running the department. Mayor Shuto already signed the legal paperwork before they put his family into the witness protection program.

"The big elephant in the room also needs to be addressed. You're wondering if I know that you, Andros, are indeed a vampire that only feeds on wildlife. You've faithfully served the police department and have become a big asset in the department. So, I know that you're a vampire. Allie, who received several accommodations for bravery and the protection of fellow citizens of Miami Florida. They were very saddened to lose you to my department. I'm aware of that your true identity is that of a mermaid. Eric, whom I've known for several years and who has faithfully served the department for years. You my man, are a very special individual and also a very big asset to our department. I'm aware that you've agreed for the betterment of human kind, to become the first historical hybrid that is a combination of vampire, werewolf and merman, which has never been done in the history of the world. I've had a long talk with Ned, Victor and the one you call Big Lou. So, I've addressed that I know your true identities and existence. Having those powers will prove useful currently and going forward as you continue to serve the Bangor Police Department."

"Phew, I was wondering if you would ever find out. Sir, this case has proven to be one of the biggest cases in my career."

"Outside the department, please call me Harry. Calling me sir makes me feel older that I really am."

"How long have you known?"

"Remember, when you were going through your transformation? Right after the experiment took place? Ned and Victor and eventually Big Lou came to visit me. Why do you think I authorized some of the time off? I already knew, young man. They made me sign a non-disclosure agreement telling me I can never disclose your true identities. They also made me do a blood vow with all of them promising the same. So, trust me, my life depends on keeping your secret. I'll take it to my grave. In other words, your secrets are safe with me. I want to assure all of you that I'll never disclose anything to anyone. I've just spilled my guts. Lieutenant Bane, you're the lead in this investigation. Yes, I'm in command but you're the lead on this case. What do you want to do next?"

"Harry, we've been very busy with the case the last couple of days. I think that we need to have a big dinner at my house. All of us need to recharge our batteries and get to know one another. I'm sure that Evan and his group will be OK for at least one evening. My dad has a staff that will prepare a meal fit for members of royalty. What do you say, old sport?"

"I'm in agreement and haven't had a decent meal in days. I'm also a Kung Fu instructor at my own dojo. I'm a seventh-degree black belt in that art. I'm OK if my lead lieutenant is with OK with having dinner at your family's farm. What do you say Eric?"

"I hate hospitals, let's get the hell out of here then head to your farm. Harry, if I may call you that, please follow us in my Charger."

"You got it, Eric."

"I can second that motion my love," Allie said as she watched Eric's butt, walking out behind him as they left the hospital.

Allie, Andros and Eric walked to the car. He opened the driver's side door then she jumped in. She had a smile on her face. Eric knew that she liked to drive his car. He got into the passenger side then buckled his seat belt. Andros got into the backseat but was on his cell. They knew he was getting the staff at the farm ready for the everyone's arrival. Allie turned the car over then listened to it purr. Eric looked back to see the chief driving his 1989 Ford truck. Allie opened the window to enjoy some fresh air coming into the car. She peeled out the parking lot with Harry following right behind her. Within twenty minutes, everyone made it to the Andros family farm.

Victor walked right out then met the chief with open arms. The staff always seemed to be very welcoming of guests showing up at the farm. He had some sirloin steaks placed on the barbecue for Harry and Allie. Everyone got out the cars then went inside. The staff had a vintage 1988 white wine for their pleasure. Andros decided to be the host. He and the staff pulled chilled wine glasses then graciously poured each one a sample of the wine. Eric seemed to relax a little and put his guard down. Allie seemed to be also relaxed. Due to the high stress of the job, it seemed to be a welcome treat. In the back of his mind, Eric just wanted to save the sheriff. Allie knew what his thoughts were. She cautioned him with her mind to stop thinking about the case and live a little. The chief seemed to be warming up to the family of Andros. Just before the steaks were ready, both Andros and Eric suddenly stopped speaking and become very quiet. Allie realized something was up so she immediately pulled them aside.

"What's going on? Why aren't you trying to enjoy

life for once?"

"I'll speak for both of us. Whenever a human is being maimed or harmed, a vampire can sense it. Something is telling me that Evan is about to make a move on Clyde. Harry, you'll have to come with us?"

"Eric, do you know where they are at this exact moment, old sport?"

"On your land, there's an ancient burial ground that used to be used by the local tribes of Bangor. In my thoughts, I'm visualizing two stone buildings that are right next to each other. Do you know where I'm talking about?"

"Yeah, it's about ten miles east of our home. Our respect for the dead has kept us from going there. What you're describing sounds like that's the place."

"I can also see that they have the poor sheriff bound between two cars. In front of him, his hands are bound with rope. They have the rope tied to the hitch of an old cop car. His feet are also bound with rope and tied to the hitch of an old farming truck."

"I've been listening to all of you. We need to get to this place right away. If the sheriff is being harmed or maimed, our duty is to protect him."

"It might be dangerous Harry. We can go to stop them."

"Eric, if Evan is the one directing the harm, you'll need me to fight him. Let's get out asses up there now."

"We have the ability to fly there. Clyde maybe

already dead or badly injured if we drive there, old sport."

"You need to go. Don't worry, my staff will keep the dinner waiting for all of you. Please go now!" Victor said with an escalated tone.

ERIC, ANDROS, ALLIE AND Harry walked out of the family home. Harry ran to his truck then got the totem to assist him. He sprinted back to the front of the house. Eric transformed into a vampire. Not much changed with the exception of his eyes, which were totally black. His skin turned a ghostly white color. Blood vessels made themselves known in his forehead. Blood-soaked fangs came out the sides of his mouth. Andros also transformed and looked very similar to Eric. An expression of fear came to Harry's face but he did his best to be open to all of them. Eric grabbed Allie's arm then jumped in the air. It sounded like a bolt of thunder as they both vanished out of sight. Andros grabbed Harry by the arm, then bolted into the air. They both looked like nothing but blur. Before Harry could realize what was going on they landed just outside the ancient burial ground.

They hid behind a big rock. Eric always liked to have a meeting to discuss strategy before a fight. The ancient writings on Harry's walking stick began to shine brightly, which meant that Evan was up to something. He knew that Evan would use every tool at his disposal. To their dismay, the ropes binding the sheriff were tightened. Both cars were about to pull him apart.

Harry got a very pissed off look at his face. Due to how big Evan stood, Eric decided to transform into a werewolf.

His body begun to contort. His nose vanished then a big snout came in his place. His arms and legs vanished then big paws with razor sharps claws came in its place. Saliva dripped from the big fans of mouth. His height bolted up to eight foot two. A look of horror and fear came over Harry's face as he watched this happen.

"Don't worry Harry, Eric will not harm you. He's simply getting ready for battle against Evan."

"How do you want to go about this, old sport?"

"If we rush toward Evan, he'll have his two guys peel out then split Clyde in two," he said as saliva dropped off his big pearly white werewolf fangs.

"With our lighting fast speed,Eric and I could cut the ropes. It will leave us exposed to be attacked by both Evan and his crew."

"Allie and I will help you fight them. Please go and save Clyde's life."

Eric grabbed Harry's arm then took off like a bolt of fire toward the front to stop injury to his arms. Andros did the same after grabbing Allie by the arm. Within a micro second, Eric was the first to cut the ropes off of Clyde's arm making the front of him drop of the ground. Andros came in right behind him then cut the ropes off his feet. This caused him to fall to the ground. With the reflexes of a cheetah, Allie grabbed up Clyde then bolted from a safe distance. Evan transformed into his Viking size and attire. Eric got on all fours ready to pounce at the slightest provocation from Evan. Harry begun to chant an ancient ritualistic spell. The totem or walking stick shined brightly with blinding white aura.

"By the powers of Oden, I hereby strip you of the ancient powers of a Viking."

"You are no match against me."

Just as he tried to lift his doubled sided battle ax, he dropped it to the ground. The other guys working for Evan sped off only leaving him with a defeated look on his face. As big as he was, he threw the battle ax to the ground. He got on his knees then put his hands above his head.

By this time, a helicopter hovered above then landed near them. It had the FBI emblem painted on its left side. Harry pulled out his handcuffs then rushed toward Evan. He quickly cuffed Evan with his hands behind his back.

"Evan Solcareh, you are under arrest for assault and attempted murder against Sheriff Clyde Smith. You have the right to remain silent, if you give up that right all of what you say will be held against you in a court. You have the right to an attorney. If you can't afford an attorney, the City of Bangor Maine will appoint you one at low cost. Do you understand these rights as I've disclosed them to you? Are you willing to give a statement at this time?"

"No, I invoke my right to be silent."

The agents in the helicopter swarmed Evan. They

put him inside the helicopter, which quickly took off with the prisoner into an undisclosed location. Eric transformed back into human form. Andros did the same. A look of relief came over Harry's face as they met between the two stone buildings. Clyde Smith sighed a big breath of relief as he sat down. Andros blocked his ability to hear as they discussed what just happened.

"This situation could've turned into a real shit storm, if you know what I mean, boss."

"You bet it could Eric. Andros and Allie and yourself did very well. We were able to arrest Evan without loss of life. That I'm very glad for. To be honest, your transformation into a werewolf scared the living shit out of me. It was also honorable of how much restraint you showed in what just went on. You are truly a very special and needed asset to the Bangor Police Department. Hats off to you, mate!"

Andros snapped his fingers then everyone vanished from the ancient burial ground and reappeared in the living room of the family farm. Victor placed a veil of forgetfulness over Clyde's mind. He made him forget about seeing Eric, Andros and Allie. His last memory of him being in the hospital. The feds came in then took him immediately to a safe house with medical capabilities for his needs. Eric seemed to be weakening as they continued on. Harry knew that he needed to feed. Andros, Eric and Allie left to take care of his needs.

Victor's kitchen staff brought a big sirloin steak fresh

off the barbecue for Harry. A look of extreme hunger came over his face. His stomach gave off a big GROWL! He smiled as they sat at the kitchen table. Victor smiled as he watched him devour the meal. The staff brought in a big chef's salad with blue cheese dressing. Victor poured him a chilled glass of wine.

"Harry, what you've just witnessed must never be disclosed to any living soul. It's important especially for Eric."

"Victor, I totally understand the need for secrecy. One thing that I want to make clear. I'll never disclose anything that I've seen. What surprised me during all of this was his demeanor. He could've cut Evan into a several pieces. Both of them could've killed him and be justified in doing so. This just makes me very proud of him."

"He's developed into a very wise creature. He's adhered to every rule that we've asked him to do so. It's my hope that both Allie and Andros will continue on this same path. There is a lot of work to be done, Victor."

"His time in the mortal world is very numbered. There's a lot of work to do in our world also. He'll continue to serve your department but do understand that it'll not be much longer before he's needed to serve the vampire and werewolf world."

"I do understand that. Eric will serve anybody. He's only going to do what he wants. It'll be his choice as to what he decides."

"The only question that I have is to what world that

he'll serve. The vampire world will need him. The werewolf population will also require his help in the future against to the blood rage infected werewolf members of the Wabanaki Nation. He'll also be needed to serve the aquatic world. Ned, I'm sure, will need to his help in serving the mermaid and mermen population. That young man has a very difficult decision in the future."

"You bet he does. Whatever, he decides, you and I are going to support him in whatever that decision is."

An hour later, Harry said his goodbyes then drove home. He needed to get adequate rest for all of the occurrences of today. Eric finished all the feeding needed. They all met at his house. Andros enjoyed a beer with him then took off back to the family farm. That left Allie and him to the house themselves.

CHAPTER SEVEN
"ETERNAL AQUATIC BOND"

ALLIE RAN INTO HER bedroom to take a quick shower. Eric, bloody from his feeding, did the same in his bedroom. A half hour later, they met up only wearing shower robes in the living room. Her big bodacious boobs were wanting to fall out of her robe. This naturally excited Eric. They both dropped their robes. Their mouths both gaped open with lustful desires for one another. She walked up to them then got on one knee then grabbed his left hand.

"Eric, this case will be ongoing for a long time. I can't wait for another minute. Will you marry me for time and all eternity?" she said as she pulled a huge diamond ring out of her robe, which was on the floor.

"Before I answer that we need to discuss a couple of things. You do realize that I'm a mixture of three creatures. You'll be dealing with that for the rest of your life. I'll need to feed both the vampire and werewolf inside of me."

"I do realize that my love. I accept you for whatever you are. I want to be your wife. As a team, we'll deal with those needs as they come."

"If that's the case, I do want to be your husband for all time and eternity," he said as he placed the wedding ring on his finger.

He got on one knee then also pulled a huge diamond ring out of his robe then placed it on her wedding finger. He then got up then they embraced each other. Her bodacious tits mashed against his chest as they kissed passionately for a moment. Their breathing and heartbeat increased as they continued to hold each other.

"Please realize that I want to make love you like an enraged mermaid. But it's forbidden, we can only make love when we're married."

"A big boner like this is a terrible thing to waste."

"I do realize that but we both need to show restraint in order to honor our aquatic traditions."

"How do you want to plan the wedding? Where do you want to get married. Do you still want to live in our family home? Just a lot of questions for you, my love."

"The wedding needs to be held in Ned's kingdom. Victor and everyone else will of course be invited. As for where I want to live, wherever you live is where I live. Also, realize that we can't delay the wedding much. Once a mermaid proposes, there will be only three days before the bond expires and can't reoccur for one hundred earth years. I'm certainly not going to wait a hundred years to be your wife."

"Let's plan this right away. Everything on the case will just have to be set on the back burner. I'm only sad that my mom and dad will not be here for our wedding."

"Maybe my father will be able to help us with that."

"I sure hope so."

Eric and Allie spent the rest of the evening just enjoying each other's company. He found a bottle of 1987 vintage wine that he'd forgotten about. He quickly found some chilled glasses. They looked at each other with love and admiration. Before they knew it, Allie told him she needed to some rest. He escorted her to her bedroom then kissed her good night. Eric quickly toddled himself to his own bed. Sleep felt very inviting. He curled up in his bed then fell fast asleep.

Eric and Allie spent the new couple of days inviting everyone to the wedding. Ned and Allie's mother Kay were excited to hear of the upcoming vows. Andros informed all of his family of whom would attend. The word got to Big Lou, he of course invited all of the council to attend the wedding including some friends that were werewolves that also followed the code of conduct. Harry of course accepted the invitation to attend the ceremony. Ned's kingdom had all of the mermaids and mermen get the location ready. Before they knew it, the time came for them to marry.

Andros and his family accommodated all of the invited guests to the farm. Eric felt a little nervous but the butterflies were normal for the man right before his nuptials. Allie seemed very relaxed and ready to be Eric's wife for all time and eternity. They quickly drove to the farm only to find a huge group of people waiting for them including Harry. He quickly went and opened the door for the bride to be to get out of the car. Eric got out to greet the guests.

"Hello Victor, I'm so glad you'll be attending sir."

"I'm honored to be attending. Are you folks ready?"

NED APPEARED THEN STRETCHED out his trident toward the whole group. Golden gills formed on each side of their necks. With a voice that boomed from the heavens, he told everyone to get ready. He took the trident then hit it on the ground three times. The whole group vanished then reappeared at an undisclosed location in the ocean. The expression on Harry's face appeared to be fright but he began to calm down.

Eric's mouth gaped open as he and Allie saw hundreds of mermaids and mermen smiling on each side of the aisle. They both quickly transformed. Their legs vanished to be replaced with fins. Ned and Kay, Allie's mother, were at the top of the aisle. They both swam to stand in front of Ned and Kay. Harry smiled big as he watched both of them smile as they stopped.

"Ladies and Gentlemen, we are gathered here today in my kingdom to join this mermaid and this merman in the holy bonds of eternal marriage. If there is anyone one opposed, let he or she speak. There are no opposed."

Kay quickly handed two golden rings to Ned. He smiled as his voice boomed so the multitude of people could hear him.

"Eric, do you take Allie to be your eternal wife in the bonds of marriage?"

"I do."

"Allie, do you take Eric to be your eternal husband in

the bonds of marriage?"

"I do."

"Please place the ring on each other's fingers at this time."

"By the power invested in me from the Aquatic Gods, I now pronounce Allie and Eric, eternal husband and eternal wife. You may know kiss your bride."

Eric and Allie quickly embraced in a subtle kiss. The whole crowd cheered for them. All of them knew that there would be another transformation. Allie was the first to transform. Her hair turned into a blinding white color. Then a princess crown formed on her head. Her fin turned into a very bright green color with golden speckles. Her bosom grew twice its normal size. Allie smiled as her height grew to six foot two. Her eyes also shined brightly with a golden color. Eric stood in awe of his wife's transformation.

Ned pointed his trident toward Eric. He spun into circles another tattoo of a trident that appeared on his body to match the other one. The crown of a prince appeared on his head. His fin turned into a bright golden color with blue speckles. His already muscular body turned into twice the size. A lighting bolt came from the heavens into the ocean hitting him right between the eyes. The hair on his head turned to a golden color. Allie smiled as she knew the transformation was completed.

Ned snapped his fingers then everyone vanished and reappeared back the farm with Andros and his family.

Ned, Kay, Eric and Allie also transformed back into human form as the family and friends all smiled at them.

In the back of his mind, Eric knew that there would be a reception in their honor. *I can't wait to get her home!* he quietly thought to himself. Allie heard his thoughts an gave him a very seductive smile. The crowd knew that they wanted to be home by themselves to enjoy their wedding night. They greeted their guests then Allie got into the driver's seat of the Charger after Eric opened the door for her. She grabbed his crotch as she sat inside the driver's seat. This of course excited him. He licked his lips in anticipation of what was about to occur. Eric got inside the passenger seat then shut his door. They waved goodbye as she turned the car over to listen to its thunderous purr. She peeled rubber out of the driveway of the farm. A few moments later, they pulled into the driveway of their home as husband and wife.

"Are you ready for our wedding night?"

"You bet I am, my wife!"

They got out of the car then walked into the house. They right away noticed the house had doubled in size. The small guest room had evolved into a huge honeymoon suite. There stood a huge California king sized bed. Kay made sure there was wine chilling with glasses right beside them. The small shower had turned into a huge tub and shower combination. Eric also noticed there were jets in the tub. This made him smile big. Andros also made sure there were grapes for them to enjoy.

BANGOR MAINE MURDERS

She quickly turned the water on in the tub. The water caused a fog to come over the room. While this occurred, she quickly shed her clothes then sat on the tub. Her newly resized breasts were erect as razors. The nipples were the color of cherry blossoms from the first harvest of the season. Her pelvic area moistened and needed his attention. Her eyes were looking right at Eric as he took off his clothes. This exposed his huge monster sized cock. His balls looked full. This made her lick her lips as he walked toward her. Allie turned the water jets on. Eric stood right front of her.

Allie quickly grabbed his manhood then shoved it all the way inside of her mouth. She took her fingers then fondled his gonads, which made his body stiffen. He then took himself out of her mouth and had her lie back on the tub's edge. He quickly got on his knees then savagely put his face into her already moist and inviting pussy. Eric took her clit deep inside of his mouth then swirled it with his tongue. Allie moaned as he continued to swirl his tongue. Her body stiffened as she couldn't hold back anymore. She gushed and squirted all over his face. Almost like a mini ocean of nectar of the Gods. He licked it all up and never missed a drop. Allie moaned as she sat up then looked as his throbbing member. She then put him deep inside of her. Eric went all the way in, which made her moan and whimper wanting more. He made love to her like a wild stallion. Before he knew it, his body stiffened as he shot his load deep inside of her. They both yelled in ecstasy. He then pulled out still throbbing and having an orgasm. Eric continued to shoot hot cum all over her breasts and face.

She then turned around then got on all fours. He mounted her then pumped wildly inside of her then shot a gallon deep inside of her. They both got into the water panting like rabid wolves.

"Eric, you're a fucking beast of a husband. That was the most satisfying sex and intimacy that I've ever had."

"You're a goddess and I also concur. That was pretty fucking hot and intimate."

"How do you feel now, big boy?"

"I feel heavenly and can feel my own heartbeat in my cock. What about you?"

"My clit is still throbbing. My pussy feels like it got hit by a Mack truck," she said as she poured wine for both of them.

They made love five more times until the sun came through the window of their bedroom. Andros, Harry, Big Lou and Victor snuck in then brewed them some gourmet coffee. Eric and Allie put their noses up to smell the sweet aroma of the coffee brewing. They both took a quick shower to wash off their sticky bodies. Eric and Allie put on bathrobes then walked into the kitchen to see the others smiling big for them. Andros smiled as he handed them each a cup. Harry smiled as he saw a very satisfied expression on Eric's face.

"It's nice of you to spoil my and husband and me with such yummy coffee."

"Andros and I had Big Lou bring it from Greece. How does it taste?"

"All jokes aside. It tastes heavenly to our taste buds."

"I'm glad that you're enjoying it. Harry has a surprise waiting for you in the driveway."

"Really! What did you get for us Harry?" she asked with a big smile on her face.

They quickly walked out into the driveway. You could've knocked both of them over with a feather as their mouths gaped open in awe. There stood a vintage 1955 Chevrolet. With a candy apple metallic red for the lower part of the car. The upper part of the car had a pearl colored and shiny paint job. With a smile on Big Lou's face, he popped the hood for them to see the engine. The big beefy V8 engine almost blinded them with the shiny chrome and gold-colored parts. Victor smiled as he turned the key then revved the engine. It sounded like the galloping of horses running over a small bridge. The sound of the engine was a deep and powerful roar.

"Your county issued Charger has been turned in then replaced with this beauty. Eric and Allie do you like you're wedding gift from me?" Harry asked with a huge smile on his face.

"Hell yes, we love it, Harry!" she yelled as she looked at the huge exhaust of their new car.

Eric and Allie went inside and got dressed. Harry and the rest of the crew drove back to the farm with Andros. His family had the reception ready for them. Allie and Eric got into the Chevy then drove to the farm.

Victor had the servants cook meals for the human.

He had some vintage blood from a royal mount elk for Eric and Andros to enjoy. Harry and Big Lou had them sit down. They brought gifts for them to open. Eric smiled as he watched Allie open all the gifts for their new house together. She got a new blender, fine china plates and sterling silver forks and knives to use in their house.

Eric's eyes sparkled as Harry brought him another gift. He quickly took the wrapping paper off the gift. There stood a box made of eighteen caret gold. With a huge mile, he opened the box to find a .357 magnum pistol gold plated with an ivory handle.

"This belonged to my grandfather and it's yours my boy!"

"Oh my God, that is the prettiest gun that I've ever seen."

"It's very old but it has been refurbished for you to use on the job. It's almost like a mini cannon."

"I'm very honored Harry, thanks a million!" he yelled as he gave him a big bear hug.

CHAPTER EIGHT
"BACK TO BUSINESS"

Eric AND ALLIE SPENT the next two weeks enjoying going on a boat borrowed by Harry. He served as captain as they put out lobster traps. They caught their limit then donated their catch to charity.

It was also time for them to get back to the business at hand. Harry knew he was ready to get back to work. During the time they were off work, four more murders occurred. Harry wanted them to investigate each and every one. The feds were working hard on bringing Trent to justice. The first murder Harry wanted them to investigate was that of Harry's own brother Sam. He let them know what address to go to.

Eric and Allie were just having a cup of coffee, which seemed to liven up their senses. Andros knocked on the door of their home. Allie could see in his eyes that he was hinting for a cup of coffee. She smiled as she poured him a cup. Of course, he graciously accepted her gesture of friendship.

"Old sport, are you ready to get back to work?"

"The time with my lovely wife has been great. Yes, I'm ready. How about you?"

"I've spent the extra time spending it with my family. The chief told me that were four murders since we've been off work. Has he told you which one he wants to sink our teeth into first?"

"He wants to us to investigate the murder of his

brother, Sam Montel. Allie and I have done some investigating about him already."

"What have you found out about him?"

"I'm the one that did some of the homework. Sam Montel, standing a short five foot four. His frame could be described as chiseled and huge due to his past use of steroids. Sam weighed about a solid one hundred and sixty-five pounds. He had balding black hair and dark brown eyes."

"That's a very detailed description. Have you and Eric discovered what his involvement is with the Trent Lechesky?"

"Unfortunately, Sam suffered from an addiction to sex. There are not too many working girls in this area. Trent sent very high paying escorts his way. He used a lot of them to the point he indebted himself over one hundred and fifty thousand for unpaid services. Trent sent his goons to either have him pay up or pay with his life. The latter is what's obviously happened. Harry informed us that the crime scene is secured. Sam's body is in the morgue."

"Do they know how he died? Better yet, what's the official cause of death?"

"Just like the other's he's been shot on the right temple. This caused instant death. His penis and gonads are missing from the body. His throat was also sliced with the utmost precision. There also was a vampire mask left on the side of his body. Warning, the crime scene is very bloody due to his cut throat and missing genitals. This one kind of hit the boss hard. We need to finish up our coffee and head over there. His studio apartment is on Twenty-three, Twenty-one Bangor Heights Drive, apartment One Twenty-one."

"Let's fire up our car then head over there. Like, I said it probably smells to high heaven. It's been over a week. Forewarned Andros, I know you are sensitive to bad smells," Eric said as he took his last swig of coffee.

Eric and Allie scurried into their bedroom, got dressed then met Andros by their car. He saw the joy on his wife's face as he opened the door to the Chevy. Andros eagerly jumped in the back seat and he got into the passenger side then shut his door. Within fifteen minutes they made it to Sam Montel's apartment. A junior police officer let them in after he saw their badges.

T HE AROMA WAFTING FROM the bedroom gave them a strong desire to throw up. Something told them to go into there first. The whole area appeared to have been dusted for fingerprints. The queen-sized bed, caked with a huge amount of dried blood stood before them. Allie noticed brain matter on the right side of the headboard. Also, dried seminal fluid remained on the pillow case. Eric noticed a digital wrist watch on the right side of the bed. Andros and Allie knew what was about to happen. They found neighboring chairs then sat down and closed their eyes. Eric stood while he grasped the watch to see if anything would come to mind.

Late one evening, Sam Montel was sitting in his bed and smoking a cigarette and drinking a stiff shot of vodka. He appeared to be getting ready to retire for the evening. A huge CRACK! rang out of the kitchen door window. This put Sam on immediate alert.

Two huge men made their way through the door then into the bedroom. The first one appeared to be six foot five and around two hundred pounds but walked with a small limp. He had long greasy black hair but looked like a body builder type. The second one, similar in height at around six foot two and well over two hundred pounds appeared neat and well-groomed. He had long blond hair put up in a ponytail behind his head. Both appeared to be the body builder type. Both of them drew a Glock pistol then walked towards Sam's bedroom.

"Good evening, Sam Montel. My name is Cody Graves and this is my cousin Mark Smith. It appears you've been a very greedy and bad boy using Trent Lechesky services and not paying for them. Did you think it was free, buddy?"

"No, I certainly didn't think it was free."

"You racked up over one hundred and fifty thousand dollars in unpaid sexual favors. We are men of honor. Do you have the money in your safe?"

"No, I've been trying to pull it out of my retirement to pay Trent. I just need a little more time to come up with the funds."

"You've had six months to pay up. You have to admit, he's been very patient. I'm afraid you're out of time buddy."

Just as Cody brushed his greasy black hair back, two very homely looking women walked into the bedroom. Both only wearing a robe, which they allowed to drop to the floor. Sam smiled and of course got an instant erection. Cody and Mark walked back out of the bedroom. Sam looked at them with a horrified look on his face. He also appeared bewildered that two skanky looking women were here to pleasure him. One of the women reached into her bag then pulled out a huge eighteen-inch black dildo with a harness. She immediately put on the harness then placed the dildo inside of it. The other girl pulled out a Glock pistol then pointed it right at Sam. A horrified look came over his face as they both walked up to him in the bedroom. They ripped his underwear off then ordered him to get on all fours. The Glock pistol was only within an inch of his right temple. Sam complied with their demands. Using no lube, the girl wearing the huge dildo shoved it deep inside his ass.

"Do you like that big boy?"

"I bet you're getting off on this you're a sick bastard," the girl pointing the Glock at his temple placed the pillow case underneath him to catch any fluid.

The girl wearing the dildo shoved it deeper inside of his ass. Blood started to spurt from the use of the dildo. The girl with the gun in her hand reached down then masturbated his throbbing cock. Not being able to hold anything back, he shot his load onto his own pillow case as he knelt on all fours on his bed. Both girls laughed and mocked as Cody handed them each a Bowie knife.

The girl wearing the dildo grabbed his balls then sliced them off and put them into a plastic bag. The girl with the Glock reached down then cut his limp penis off also placing it into a bag. Blood spurted from his groin area. It shot into several directions. Sam screamed in agony as he covered his empty genital area. Cody came over with his Glock then shot him in the right temple, which instantly killed him. Mark placed the vampire mask by his body. The two working girls took the bags with his genitals with them as they got dressed and left.

"I guess our job is done here Mark. Let's go back to our room at Garden Crest Hotel. I'll give Trent a call for further instructions."

"What room are we in again?"

"You dumb shit, room thirty-three. We need to get out of here before the cops show up."

Allie and Andros immediately opened their eyes. Eric did the same with a horrified look on his face. He looked down at his phone then noticed a text from Harry. Some of the junior detectives had found two Bowie knives and two Glocks in the field. They also found two nude girls with syringes in their arms apparently killed by hot shots of heroin. The prints on the guns and Bowie knives came back with prints of Cody Graves and Mark Smith known to be affiliated with the Lechesky Organization. Eric smiled as he looked up at Andros and Allie. He then looked down at his phone reading further. The SWAT team had mobilized at the hotel and was awaiting his orders.

"Apparently, we need to get our butts over to the

Garden Crest Hotel. They already have the Glocks and Bowie knives in police custody. They ran prints and just like clock work it came back to Cody Graves and Mark Smith. The SWAT team has mobilized and are ready for our orders. They also found the two working girls we saw in the vision dead from heroin shots in their arms. Their bodies are already at the morgue. Harry told me by texts that after their arrests, they are going to take custody of them and take them in for questioning. That only leaves two more goons of the Lechesky Organization that we have to capture. The chief made it abundantly clear that the hotel has been cleared of any surprise snipers all we have to do is make the arrest. We already know what room they are staying in. Let's get out of here. Allie, it's time to burn some rubber. Time is of essence per Harry."

"I couldn't agree more. Get the car and let her stretch her legs."

They all piled into the '55 Chevy. As soon as they put their seat belts on Allie put the pedal to the metal. Eric looked at the speedometer as they pulled out of Sam's residence. She pushed it to one hundred and five miles per hour. Andros held on for dear life. He had a death grip on the headrest on Allie's seat. They made it within five minutes. Harry was there to greet them. He had them all put on official police bullet proof vests.

"Harry, we already know what room they're in."

"Eric, go and make the arrests, son."

Ten SWAT members piled out of the van with shields and assault rifles. Eric decided he just wanted to breach the motel room and immediately arrest Cody and Mark. They all made their way to find both of them sleeping peacefully in their beds as they breached the room. Two of the SWAT members put them in cuffs and made them stand on their knees.

"Cody Graves and Mark Smith, you are under arrest for the rape and murder of Sam Montel. You have the right to remain silent, if you give up that right all of what you say will be held against you in a court. You have the right to an attorney. If you can't afford an attorney, the City of Bangor Maine will appoint you one at low cost. Do you understand these rights as I've disclosed them to you?" Lieutenant Bane asked with his eyes glued on Cody Graves and Mark Smith.

"We understand our rights and will not be giving a statement at this time."

"Get these pieces of human trash out of here."

"Gladly."

A helicopter from the FBI landed then immediately took them into custody. A big look of relief came over Harry's face as he patted Eric on the back for a job well done. He took off in the helicopter to escort the prisoners to an undisclosed location. Allie and Andros had a big smile on their face as they got into the car then drove to the farm of Andros's family for some needed relaxation.

CHAPTER NINE
"BLOOD RAGE"

ALLIE DROVE THEM TO the farm. Victor greeted them with a very worried look on his face. Andros looked at his father with a concerned look on his face. Eric and Allie also noticed the expression on Victor's face. They all walked into the house. In the back of all of their minds, they knew that something was wrong. Andros knew that his father would spill the beans. The house servants brought everyone a cup of gourmet coffee with fresh cream from one of the remaining cows on the farm. Eric and Allie sat on a neighboring couch. Andros sat in his normal recliner. Eric could sense with his enhanced powers that there would be trouble on the horizon. Victor walked up to the middle of the living room then placed his hand on his chin.

"Father, all of us here can sense that something is wrong. So, what's wrong?"

"Andros, Allie and Eric, something is very wrong. I know that you've been busy with your case load at work. That's why I haven't bothered you until now. Do you remember what you saw, my son, with the members of the indigenous tribes here in Bangor?"

"Yes, the members of the tribes that suffer from blood rage, why?"

"For the most part they've stayed on the reservation. They've not bothered us. The chiefs of the tribes have asked for our help. There are only four of them among the tribe. They kept them contained until now."

"What's happened to prompt our intervention?"

"They've attacked a very old and wise medicine man on the reservation. He is afflicted with blood rage, which angered the tribal leaders of all the tribes. Big Lou can tell you more. Lou, please walk in and explain."

"Hello all, I hope everyone is well. The blood rage infected werewolves have left the reservation and come on our lands and territories. They also created close to twenty-five new blood rage werewolves that openly accepted this horrid affliction. The medicine man they've attacked is the most senior member of the tribe. Normally, the council would never involve themselves in internal tribal affairs. The treaty they have with the United States is to have total autonomy. Victor and I found my eldest brother, Alfred in a field just north of here. What's left of his body is just in parts. Before he died, he bit my arm to share what happened in the attack. In my eyes and also the opinion of the council that they've crossed the line. I take my brother Alfred's murder personally. That is why I chose to seek guidance of the council. Their instructions were to disclose this to all of you. They've also instructed me that all of the tribe that suffer from blood rage must be terminated post haste. It needs to be brought to a close swiftly and delicately."

"How does the council want us to proceed? We are here to help you Big Lou," Eric said as he took a big swig of his cup of coffee, which dribbled down his chin. This made Allie smile even in a time of crisis.

"I'll need to all stand in the center of the room. I'm going to share Alfred's last moments with you then we'll come up with a plan."

Everyone finished up their coffee then walked into a circle as requested by Big Lou. This also included Victor. They all grabbed hands then closed their eyes to see Alfred's memories before he died so tragically.

ALFRED WALKED INTO A field just to enjoy some evening air. He had brought his terrier for the company. With his six-foot four frame and weighing close to four hundred pounds, he sat down then petted his dog not having a care in the world.

In the distance four native American Indians taunted their prey. They ran toward Alfred. They jumped high in the air. Before landing they all transformed in mid flight into menacing and powerful werewolves. Their eyes were solid red with the color of blood. Slobber came from their mouths as they closed in on Alfred. As Alfred stroked the head of his dog, he noticed them running at him. There was no time for him to transform for self-preservation. Without even hesitating, two of the members lunged and made contact with his body. Both of his arms were severed from his body. Blood shot from both sides with the beat of his heart. They opened their mouths with an insatiable hunger for blood. Another member looked Alfred in his eyes then bit his jugular vein. Bright red blood shot in the air to the gaping mouths of the werewolves. With their razor-sharp claws, they severed his legs and his genitals. With almost all of the blood drained from his body, two members each took a severed arm then ran off in the distance. The two remaining members consumed his genitals then each took a severed leg and ran off in the distance. All of them looked back at Alfred with their blood-stained faces and blood red eyes then a BIG HOWL! rang out from their snouts as they ran off in the distance. By this time, Big Lou had transformed and chased them but couldn't find them.

A̲LLIE, ERIC, VICTOR AND Andros let go of Big Lou's hand. A small tear of blood ran down his face as the vision ended. Victor displayed nothing but anger on his face. Andros also looked very pissed off by what had happened to Alfred. Eric sat back down on the couch placing his hand on his chin. Tears flew freely from Allie's eyes as she grasped Big Lou's hand to help with his sadness and deep kindled anger.

"Big Lou, we need to develop a plan and execute it swiftly," Victor said as he rubbed Big Lou's shoulder to sooth him.

"We have permission to terminate their lives without repercussions of violating the treaty with the tribes."

"Big Lou do you know where they're hiding out?"

"They are banished from ever entering the reservation. This is due to the death of their medicine man. It's my guess they're hiding out deep into

Manhood Mountain, which is about twenty miles east of our location. We need to develop a plan that doesn't force us to engage with them. Any of their blood would infect us."

"Manhood Mountain is a place that our family has shied away from. It's our belief that the land is cursed. I think that Eric might have an idea. He does possess some powers that we don't have. Any thoughts Eric?"

"Yes, an idea comes to mind. Ned gave me the power to call upon the elements of the earth to use against anybody that wrongly trespasses or takes a life. With my research of werewolves, they can be killed two ways. First, anything silver is fatal to werewolves. Secondly, severing the head of the werewolf is the only other way."

"Go on, what do you have in mind?"

"Is there a body of water in this place you've called Manhood Mountain?"

"Yes, there's a man-made lake built in the early nineteen forties that's still there."

"I'm going to create a wall of water then I'll turn it into liquid silver. They would have to be chased or forced to go within the wall. The silver would be as hot as liquid magma from an actual volcano. One idea would be for them to chase us. Once we run into the body of water I'll swiftly turn it into liquid silver. What do you think?"

"It sounds safe but at the same time, it's risky."

"On the other hand, it's a plan. I say we do it," Big

Lou said and his eyes brightened up.

"Victor, what do you think?"

"When somebody kills one of our own, it's our duty to seek justice for this senseless murder. I'm also in support of this plan."

"Something else that you need to know. We are not going to transform at all. They must never know of our existence. We are just going to serve as bait for them. With our enhanced powers, they'll never be able to catch us. How soon do you want to do this?"

"The council said they want it resolved quickly and swiftly. How about right now?"

"When was the last time all of you fed? Have your needs been taken care of? If not, your powers will weaken causing us to be in possible danger."

"Andros and I just fed a little while ago. How about Eric and Allie?"

"We're going to be fine. Both of us feel strong and ready to get the show on the road."

Everyone went outside to breathe in some cold Bangor Maine wind. Andros looked at Eric and Allie with vengeance in his eyes. Eric decided it was time to fly. He grabbed Big Lou's hand then bolted like a bolt of lightning. A loud CRACK! rang from the position where they stood. Andros took Allie's hand then did the same. Victor instructed the house crew to keep things safe. He then turned into nothing but a blur as he took off after the rest of the crew.

Seconds later, they arrived in a grove of trees near the lake. Andros and Eric noticed right away the blood rage werewolves were sitting by a roaring fire. The feeling of evil made the hair on the back of Eric and Allie's neck as they got closer. He sized up the body of water. Eric would be the only one to transform in order to use his powers. Eric and Allie sneaked into the lake to set the snare for the trap. Victor, Big Lou and Andros then quietly walked toward them. Showing they had balls as big as church bells. Eric transformed then a big trident appeared in his arm. He pointed it toward the water making it vanish. Allie noticed a small grove of trees. There were four side by side each other. She signaled to him that would be the best place to set the trap. Victor decided to start the action.

"Hey assholes, did you like picking on the small guys?"

"We are going to tear you to shreds. My boys and I are going to enjoy devouring your whole body and smile doing it."

LIKE GREASED LIGHTNING, A big BANG! rang out as all twenty-nine of them jumped into air. In mid flight they transformed into blood thirsty werewolves. Victor, Andros and Big Lou took off with their legs turned into nothing but a blur. Eric directed the body of water then placed a wall of water in front of the trees. Andros, Big Lou and Victor quickly ran through the body of water. The trident on Eric's chest shined and burned like wild fire. The water quickly transformed into hot liquid silver. Victor and Andros taunted them, yelling at them to come and get them. All of them ran toward what they thought was water. All twenty-nine werewolves entered the body of liquid silver at the same time. All of them screamed and gave out a big HOWL! that would burst anybody's ear drum. The smell of burning flesh and hair wafted its way toward Big Lou, Victor and Andros. This made all of them bend over an immediately throw up. The smell of death left. Eric recalled the water then placed it back into area from where it came. Eric then collapsed into Allie's arms. The trident on his chest stopped shining. Big Lou saw this then immediately ran to assist Allie. Ned appeared in the body of water.

"Eric will be just fine. I have to take him into my personal chambers. My daughter and I will be back. He called upon an ancient power that's rarely used."

Allie, Eric and Ned quickly vanished out of Manhood Lake. Victor decided to snap his fingers then everyone vanished and reappeared at the steps of the house on the farm. Big Lou had a very worried look on his face. Andros also noticed that he appeared very weak. Victor and Andros both knew that he needed to feed to restore his strength. Victor alerted the house staff to get one of the cattle ready.

CHAPTER TEN
"CRIMSON TIDE"

ANDROS TOOK A VERY Big Lou out in the field for him to feed. Victor had a genuine look of concern toward his old friend, as Victor, Andros and Big Lou went out in the field.

Eric and Allie appeared good as new. They knew that Big Lou was about to feed. Eric smiled then ripped his clothes off and transformed into a werewolf. This made Big Lou smile as Victor had one of the house staff bring another cow for him to feed on. A loud POP! rang out and blood and sinew transformed Eric into a hulking and menacing werewolf. Andros opened the gate to have the two cows go out to feed in the neighboring pasture. Saliva dripped from Big Lou's snout and he got on all fours then ran with a fury toward one of the cows. A big HOWL! came from Eric as he followed Big Lou. With razor sharp claws, Big Lou lunged at the cow. A big THUD! rang out as he tore the cow in half then feasted on all the blood, innards and bone. Eric also tore into his cow with a vengeance, tearing it into pieces and enjoying the blood and sinew as if it was his last meal. Victor, Andros and Allie smiled as they watched contently.

Forty minutes later, Eric and Big Lou transformed back into human form. Victor had the house staff bring them clothes to cover their masculine bodies. Harry pulled up in his car. He wanted to make sure all was well with everyone. *Usually, when Harry comes it*

126

means more work for us, Eric thought to himself. *I'd agree with you, my husband,* Allie said back to him with her thoughts. Victor directed everyone to walk into the house. The staff pulled out a vintage cognac for them to enjoy. He also knew Harry would come bearing news for them. The cognac imported from Greece, was a good year, a 1981 vintage. Harry sat at the end of the table, while Eric and Allie sat next to him on each side. Victor sat down on the opposite end. The staff graciously poured cognac for all to enjoy.

"What brings you to our farm?"

"It's been a while since I've heard from any of you. Your assumption is correct, some very specialized work came across my desk."

"What kind of work?" Eric asked as he sipped on his warm cognac.

"With a lot of surveillance, my junior detectives found out some very valuable information."

"With the utmost respect sir, stop beating around the fucking bush! Please tell us sir."

"With our informants at the marina, we've discovered that Trent and Alex Lechesky decided to visit Bangor Maine. Scuttlebutt is they're pretty tired of not getting a return on their investment with the mafia's money."

"What does that have to do with us? Eric and I know that the feds are handling that side of this brutal case."

"You're correct on that Allie. However, they've reached out to our agency because they created a task force for the mission dubbed as Crimson Tide. We've also been informed that Trent and Alex are also transporting a huge amount of cocaine for the drug users here in Bangor. This triggered involvement with the DEA and CIA. It's going to be a huge task force. They've decided to travel by boat due to the risks involved in flying. The Coast Guard informed us they're traveling by a huge cruise liner with a barge being towed right behind them.

"He is also bringing an army of mercenaries to assist them in their attempt to collect funds. Sadly, they also have a huge amount on explosive material such as C4 and many other products. This is also triggered the involving of the ATF. So, you see it's going to be group effort. Our efforts may close the case. All of his workers have been recalled back to Chicago. In a nutshell, it's going to be up to us to finally close the door on this case. It'll not bring back the lives of those we lost during this case but it'll bring closure."

"What's your take on our involvement sir? Also, who is going to be in charge on our end of Crimson Tide?"

"I'll be the commander, but Eric, you'll be in charge of the execution of the mission."

"How much time do we have to prepare for their arrival?"

"Judging by what's been reported by the marina, Trent, Alex and his crew should be here within two days. ATF, FBI and DEA with be aboard a Coast Guard vessel that's due to arrive here in the morning."

"That doesn't give us much time, sir."

"Usually in a mission of this caliber there never is enough time. It'll be the biggest mission that Bangor Police Department has ever taken on. Also, I fully expect that Victor, Big Lou and all of your family must help in the arrest of Trent and Alex. I've also chosen to involve our SWAT team and the explosive experts. I'm sure that Trent and Alex plan to blow Bangor Maine off the face of the earth."

"Do you have any plans as to our first step in this case?"

"The marina has every available SWAT member and police officer watching it. As far as the involvement, I also need to give you some very bad news. Then I'll tell you where I think we should start. At eight thirty this morning, five small missiles have blown up the entire building that houses our police department into a pile of rubble. Twenty-five people dead including our police commissioner, Mandy Phillips. The mayor, based on Bangor's City Charter has immediately appointed me as Interim Commissioner until a replacement can be found or I accept the appointment on a permanent basis."

"Holy shit boss! My father and Mandy's parents went to school together. She'll be missed and you're right, every one of our fallen heroes deserves to be avenged. Phew, I'm so glad that you weren't at your office when this occurred. You're also going to be in danger sir."

"Yes, my safety is very much at stake. Victor, may I stay on your farm until this all blows over?"

"You bet. Andros and I have plenty of room for you. Big Lou is going to call on his five brothers from Greece. Andros and his siblings will also assist in the capture of these pieces of shit!"

"The father of all vampires has also been alerted of what's going on," Andros said as he took a sip of the last of his cognac.

"Who is the father of all vampires?" Eric asked with his eyebrows raised.

"You wouldn't believe me if I told you."

"Stop pussy footing around! Who's coming?"

"OK you've asked for it. Count Dracula is flying in from Transylvania as we speak."

"I thought he was long since dead."

"No, the father of all vampires is very much alive. One of his servants has brought him back. There are two more people that are also in route to us."

"You've got me curious. Who else is coming to help us in the case?"

"King Lycaon, the very first known werewolf. Dubbed as the father of all werewolves. He's been living in seclusion in Greece for many years. You'll also feel that I'm feeding you a line of shit when I tell you who the last person that is in route to us."

"You're killing us and leaving us in suspense. Who the hell is also coming?"

"Frankenstein himself is also in route to us. Most people thought he was just a myth or fairytale but that's the farthest from the truth. He's very much alive and has lived in Greece also in seclusion. He's been made an honorary member of the council."

"Holy Shit! We are going to have the help of our forefathers to help us bring a close to this case."

"My father Ned and two of his cabinet members will also be here."

"Are you sure you're be able to house all of these famous members of our inner circle?"

"Yes, we've got plenty of room. It's going to be a big honor to house all of these people. Especially, housing the count. That's going to be a divine pleasure on our family's part."

"Is the count aware of our code of conduct? Not to harm any humans in any way shape or form?" Allie asked as she finish the last of her cognac.

"The count and every member of his crew informed us they'll honor our code of conduct."

"Harry, this is going to be one hell of a fight!" Andros yelled as he finished the last of his cognac.

"I'd agree with you. It's going to be like World War Three is coming to Bangor Maine."

CHAPTER ELEVEN
"SUPERNATURAL GODS"

ERIC, ALLIE AND ANDROS just sat there with their mouths gaping open in amazement. They also had fear of the loss of lives that might occur.

Within a wrinkle in time, the thundering sounds of big helicopters came to the farm. A huge THUD! rang out as the first helicopter landed. Victor and Andros rushed out to meet the passengers. A man with long black hair got out first. Eric and Allie also came out to observe. This man wore rose colored sunglasses. In the light, he blue black hair glistened. He wore a big blood colored diamond on his finger. He wore a big top hot, which had gone out of style years ago. This stranger stood around six foot tall and just looked to be a very lean one hundred and eighty pounds. Victor and Andros immediately fell to their feet then kissed the ring on his finger. *That must be the father of all vampires,* Eric thought to himself. *I would agree, Eric,* Allie answered him back with her thoughts.

The count informed Victor and Andros that he wanted to meet the hybrid right away. Many other vampires carrying rifles walked right beside him as he promptly made his way toward Eric and Allie. Both of their breathing rapidly increased as they were about to meet the man that created all vampires. In the supernatural circles, he could be looked at as a god. He motioned the guards to back off as he walked toward them. He walked with a slight limp. The count used a walking sticking painted black with a sterling silver bat on the very top. As he walked up to Allie, he gently grabbed her hand then kissed it. He then kissed her on both cheeks, which is customary for people from foreign lands.

"Hello Madame, I'm Count Dracul but people in this country call me Count Dracula."

"The honor is all mine your highness," she said as she knelt down then kissed his ring.

Count Dracul greeted Eric with the same gesture. He kissed then left cheek of his face then the right cheek.

"You must the hybrid that Victor and Andros have told me so much about. I'm Count Dracul."

"It is I, the man that has vampire, werewolf and merman DNA mixed. It's a divine honor to meet you, your highness," Eric said as he knelt down then kissed his ring.

"To many people in my inner circle, they say it's preposterous to mix the breeds of creatures. I felt very skeptical myself. However, here you are my son, in all your glory. The honor is all mine sir. We have come to assist you in your fight against the mob. We also did it to show our support of your kind and race," he said as he peered over his rose-colored glasses with eyes the color of blood.

"Your Highness, let me take you inside of the house. Other guests are do to arrive any second."

Victor and Andros followed the count and all of his body guards into the house. A big THUD! rang out as all the other helicopters landed on the farm. A big HOWL! rang out from the next helicopter. Big Lou, Victor, Andros and Eric ran to greet the next arriving guests.

A huge man standing close to seven feet tall wearing a three-piece suit was the first to walk out of the helicopter. His face bore scars of former stitches down the middle of his face and on the top of his head. There were two metal prongs sticking outside each side of his neck. Eric sized him to be around four hundred pounds of a very sturdy frame. He had one eye that was almost white in color. While the other eye looked to be dark brown. Allie noticed he was wearing platforms that were around seven inches. Eric noticed he was completely bald but his face had an expression of a very wise soul. He also was very interested in meeting the hybrid. This stranger pushed his bodyguards aside to get to Eric. He appeared very nervous to meet this creature. Eric went at it with a very open and mature mind.

"You must be the hybrid that everyone is talking about. It's an honor to meet such a unique creature. I'm a mixture of several human body parts. I assure you that I have a very wise and old soul that resides in this body. My name is Frankenstein but all of my friends and family called me Frankie. I've been residing in Greece for hundreds of years. I'm also an honorary member of the vampire council."

"Mr. Frankenstein, it is I, the man who has vampire,

werewolf and mermen DNA in my body. My name is Eric Bane and this is my wife, Allie Bane."

"Please call me Frankie. The honor is all mine kind sir."

Victor and Andros quickly walked with Frankie and his bodyguards into the house. Another big thunderous HOWL! ran out from the last helicopter. A man standing at lease seven foot and half inches tall walked toward Eric and Allie. POUND! POUND! with each of his steps. It sounded like thunder coming from the heavens. Big Lou and Eric immediately fell to their knees to meet the very first werewolf and kiss the ring on his finger. Allie noticed that he was very eager to meet her husband.

"You must the hybrid that Victor and Andros have told me much about. My name is King Lycaon. You can call me Alfred, that is my earth given name."

"It is I, the man that has vampire, werewolf and merman DNA mixed. It's a divine honor to meet you, your highness. My name is Eric Bane and this is my wife, Allie Bane."

"We all came as a show of support. My crew is also aware that you're about to engage in a huge battle with the mob. We are all here to assist you in any way that our group can."

Eric and Allie followed Alfred and all of his bodyguards into the house. Eric and Allie felt a little intimidated due to all of the powerful beings that were now in their presence. Victor and the servants did what they could to house them. Andros had an expression on his face of being awe struck about the current beings inside of his family's house. Harry messaged to let them know that the ATF, FBI and DEA arrived and had already set up a command center. Ned arrived with several other men who snuck in like thieves in the night.

"Ned, you're always famous for arriving like a thief in the night," Victor said with a huge smile on his face.

"My group and I only came as a show of support for my daughter and son in law. I'm here to assist in any way that I can."

Victor, Andros and Ned decided to serve as hosts to all the members of supernatural royalty.

CHAPTER TWELVE "OPERATION CRIMSON TIDE"

ERIC, ALLIE, BIG LOU and Victor decided to walk outside to develop a plan and bring the closure to Crimson Tide.

"We need to develop a plan. There are a lot of spokes in the wheel so to speak. I'm wondering how we should go about bringing this case safely to a close."

"Eric, I couldn't agree with you more. Here's my two cents worth on this matter. Trent and Alex Lechesky are going to come to Bangor Maine with a very methodical and calculated approach. They're bringing drugs here, which tells me that our idea that they were going to blow Bangor off the map is not correct. They plan on doing more of the mob's business here. With all the fire power and crew to back that up, they plan on getting their money back. My gut tells me that they're going to send some military grade small subs to come to our shore first. It's my opinion that they're not going to park in the marina. They're going to drop anchor then send subs and boats into Bangor Maine. I also think that Trent and Alex are never going to step foot on the grounds of Bangor. They're going to send their minions over to do all of the dirty work. If you want to arrest them, it'll have to occur on their liner," Andros said as he leaned on the porch wall.

"That still doesn't tell how we can approach this. It's

my goal that there will not be a lot of bloodshed. That's not going to be very easy by any description of the word."

"I'm sure the feds will have the marina and the surrounding area locked down. It'll be their goal to protect Bangor. I think we should send Count Dracula and his staff on the east side of Bangor. That area is mostly land and only a small body of water resides in that area. I also think that we should send Alfred and his crew along with Big Lou on the west side. The same would apply to that area. I'll take all of the brothers including my father to the south side. The only vulnerable place that I see would be the north side. This is because that is where most of the water is. It's also very close to the marina. I think we should send Ned, Allie and Eric in that area. Frankie and his crew will handle the middle of Bangor. That would cover most of Bangor. We'd have to supply all of them with weapons and whatever else they needed to get the job done. What do you think about that Eric?" Andros asked as he rubbed his chin to make him feel more at ease.

"That sounds like a very feasible, cautious and smart plan. The only thing I'm afraid of are the explosives. Harry told us they're being a hell of a lot of it."

"Eric, we'll just have to deal with that any way that we can."

"My husband does have a valid point. How are we going to protect ourselves and the citizens of Bangor Maine?"

"We should have the SWAT team that I'm sure Harry

has already dispatched to use weapons to intercept any small rockets from reaching the shores of Bangor."

"I'm aware that the SWAT team has some surface to air missiles that could stop anything they fire at us," Allie said as she rubbed her husband's leg.

"There's a Navy SEALS team on loan to Bangor courtesy of Uncle Sam. I'm going to send teams to assist in this plan in every area that you've mentioned previously," Harry said as he took a swig of grape soda.

"You always make a sneaky appearance. You almost scared the shit of out me, boss," Eric said with a smile on his face.

"What do you think of our plan? Does it sound feasible to you?"

"It's a very solid plan to a very complicated operation to close the door on the Lechesky tyranny. As the commander of Operation Crimson Tide, I give my stamp of approval. I'll do my job as the commissioner to brief all of the other parties and agencies involved."

"The only question that I have is how to arrest Trent and Alex. I value what Andros told us. They are going to stay on the ship and never step foot on shore. Going aboard their vessel might be a little dicey, if you know what I mean."

"You're forgetting, I have the power to temporarily suspend time," Victor said as he brought out a beer for everyone to enjoy."

"Father, if anything happened to you, I'd never forgive myself."

"Andros, you need not worry about me. I might be old but I'm not dead. We could go aboard their ship, suspend time then take Trent and Alex under cuffs and chains to the shore. Once we have them on lock down, I'll restart time then you can officially arrest those bastards. They've caused nothing but murder and heartache to this once peaceful place to reside for me and my family."

"What do you think Harry? Is it OK if Victor comes with us to arrest them?"

"Victor, you're a very wise and intelligent man. If you have the power to suspend time like you say you do, I would put my stamp of approval on him helping you."

"Thanks for you support Harry. I'm sure with all of what we have. This case will be closed swiftly and efficiently."

"I'm concerned about my father's safety. He tends to go at some of his duties with a horns down ass up type of approach. I sure hope he'll think before he acts," Allie said with a worried look on her face.

"I'm sure Ned will be able to hold his own my dear," Eric said as he rubbed her shoulders to soothe her.

Meanwhile back with Alfred, Big Lou and the rest of the crew on the west side of Bangor Maine…

ALFRED, AND BIG LOU QUICKLY made their way to the west side of Bangor Maine. They were met with a Navy SEALS team and also members of the DEA. They were in awe of Alfred's appearance. With his keen sense of vision, Alfred saw two portable subs making their way with cargo and weapons. Big Lou noticed that the Navy SEALS team was ready to pounce like a lion upon his or her prey. There were over twenty men with machine guns pointing in that direction. Big Lou knew they must never reach the small dock.

One of the Navy SEALS members said to brace for impact. With Alfred's keen sense of hearing, he heard and loud WHIRLING! sound as a small missile made its way toward them. He noticed they were shooting at them with a portable missile launcher. It was time to take action. Big Lou could tell that Alfred seemed ready to make his move. The Navy SEALS team and the DEA agents had other ideas. Using binoculars, they noticed several black bags, which they assumed were drugs. Harry had informed Alfred and Big Lou that Uncle Sam had authorized deadly force if needed. As time progressed, the assailants were within fifty feet of the small dock. Two of the Navy SEALS team members prepped their missile launchers then waited for the green light to fire upon command.

A very clean-shaven Navy SEALS officer gave them a big thumbs up. Ten other Navy SEALS team members loaded their machine guns. A loud POP! rang out as three surface to ground missiles shot at the oncoming subs. A loud WHIRLING! sound rang out as they could hear the small missiles making their way toward them. Rapid GUNFIRE! rang out as they shot at the assailants. Alfred and Big Lou quickly covered their ears from hearing gun shells expelling as they continued to shoot. A loud explosion occurred as the surface to air missiles made contact with their intended targets. Several explosions occurred with body parts flying way up into the air. A Coast Guard vessel came right behind the wreckage to clean up and collect all evidence from the scene.

Meanwhile back with Eric, Allie, Andros and Victor in Bangor Maine...

"I'VE BEEN INFORMED THE route on the west side has been resolved. Count Dracula has reported they didn't take any actions on the east side. Frankie has informed us that there is also no action in his area first. All other areas show no activity that tells me they only chose to make entry on the west side only. All of the teams have assembled on the north side."

"I've heard from my brother that again no action on their end. It's time for you, Allie and Victor to do your part of this mission."

"Yeah, I would agree with my son. Its time, don't you think Eric?"

"It sounds a little dicey and I'm also worried about my wife's safety."

"I understand you, Eric. Our actions will save many lives. It will also allow Bangor Maine to become a safe haven and good place to live like it should be."

"OK, I'm going to transform into merman. Allie, please do the same. Victor and Andros will be able to follow us. Golden gills will allow them to breath."

"My father and the rest of the crew are all waiting on us."

"When I snap my fingers, all of us will vanish from here then reappear in the water right by their yacht. Be aware that I can't suspend time for a long period of time. Our actions must be swift, quick and efficient. Do you understand me?"

"Yes, I understand."

"Harry told me that once you arrest them, the DEA, FBI, ATF and the Navy SEALS team will take federal custody of them. They have a Coast Guard vessel very close by and will arrive when we need them."

"Sounds like a plan to me."

Allie and Eric took flight into the air. Victor held on for dear life as he held Allie's arm. With a terrified look on his face, Andros did the same. In midair, Allie and Eric quickly transformed into merpeople.

Allie, Eric, Andros and Victor splashed down next to the Lechesky yacht. Located twenty miles off shore…

ALL OF THEM LANDED safely in the water far enough away from the yacht to avoid detection. Victor looked at Eric to have him give the signal to stop time. He gave a big thumbs up. Victor snapped his fingers then everything stood still as a statue including the water. The only people able to move were just them. They made their way up to the ladder on the left side of the yacht and quickly boarded the vessel.

Allie with her photographic memory knew what

Alex and Trent looked like. They made their way into the captain's cabin of the yacht right on the bridge. They found Alex standing with a big cigar in his mouth. The smell of it gave Allie a strong desire to throw up in her mouth. He stood a very fat, obese five foot ten and well over four hundred and fifty pounds. Eric noticed he had balding slicked back blue-black hair. Victor noticed he had pock marks on his face from suffering from acne as a young adult. Allie noticed Trent, who appeared to be a carbon copy of his father. He stood a fat, obese five foot six and well over three hundred and fifty pounds. His hair slicked back appeared to have lice crawling off his scalp. This made Allie cringe at the very sight of these two pieces of human trash.

"Allie, do you have any handcuffs?"

"No but Victor and Andros both do."

"Hand me the cuffs."

Andros handed Eric both sets. Allie and assisted him in cuffing both men behind their backs. It was time to get them off the yacht. Harry walked in then made them jump high in the air. Victor made sure he'd be able to move with time suspended.

"When I snap my fingers, we are going to appear on the flight deck of the Coast Guard vessel."

Victor snapped his fingers then they all of them reappeared on the flight deck of the Coast Guards vessel. Eric and Andros put both men on their knees in front of him. Victor restarted time as both men had a what the hell just happened on their face.

"Why are we in handcuffs!" Alex yelled.

"*Trent Lechesky and Alex Lechesky, you are under arrest for the rape, murder and possession of drugs with the intent to distribute drugs. There will be many other charges once everything is said and done by the federal prosecutor. You have the right to remain silent, if you give up that right all of what you say will be held against you in a court. You have the right to an attorney. If you can't afford an attorney, the Unites States Government will appoint you one at low cost. Do you understand these rights as I've disclosed them to you?"* Lieutenant Bane asked them with staring daggers at them.

"All of us understand our rights. We'll be out before the ink is dry on any charges that you file against us. No, we don't wish to give a statement at this time."

"Take these pieces of human trash to jail!" Eric yelled at them.

Navy SEALS team members took both men to the brig for processing. Harry had a big smile as he watched Eric conclude Operation Crimson Tide.

"You've just closed the case. Congrats, Lieutenant Bane!"

CHAPTER THIRTEEN
"ASCENSION"

TWO WEEKS PASSED BY. Eric and Harry brought an official close to Operation Crimson Tide and all things affiliated with Trent and Alex Lechesky. All of the evidence held by the Bangor Maine Police Department was turned over to the feds. Harry with help from the insurance company had blueprints for a totally new police department headquarters. Until then, he was renting an office building for Eric, Allie, Andros and the rest of the crew to serve there temporarily

He accepted the position as the newly elected Police Commissioner of Bangor Maine. Eric accepted the role of running the police department as chief. Eric, Allie, Andros and Victor said their goodbyes to Frankie, Alfred and Count Dracula. With many thanks and an abundance of gratitude and respect for their actions. They all left then went back home. Victor decided it was time to celebrate the success of all of their actions. The fruits of their labors. Allie accepted an offer from Harry to be the assistant police chief. Everything seemed to be healing in the city of Bangor Maine. Andros accepted the full role of a deputy instead of a consultant. All of the hard work paid off in the cases. Eric and Allie were sitting in his new office having coffee. Andros walked in with his new police uniform with a grin from ear to ear. They both smiled as they viewed one of their newly vetted deputies walking with pride.

"There's been a lot of change since we closed the

case on the Lechesky stain on our community. You look very handsome Andros, I must say. "

"Thank you, Eric, or shall I say boss."

"Victor is planning a big party at your house for the closure of Operation Crimson Tide. It's my hope that things in Bangor Maine will finally calm down. Are you going to the party? Please call me Eric and not boss. I'm still part of your team, please don't forget that."

"Yes, I do plan to attend but I do have a concern to address with both of you. My instincts tell me that the mob out of Chicago will be seeking revenge or payback for us disabling their crime network here in Bangor."

"You can be rest assured they might. Remember Alex Lechesky served as one of the higher-ranking members of the mob. I'm sure it'll take them a very long time to reorganize. When they do, our department will certainly be ready for them."

A very nervous brand-new deputy knocked hard on Eric's door. Beads of sweat were rolling down his long blond curly locks.

"What can I do for you, recruit?"

"I don't know really how to tell you this," he said almost stuttering due to nervousness. "Our new police commissioner has just been shot. I just heard the call over dispatch."

"You better be careful in what you just said recruit. Please give my assistant police chief, Deputy Andros and myself more details. Where did this happen? When did this just happen? Is our commissioner still alive?"

Eric said with a glaring scowl at the new recruit.

"To answer your questions, sir and ma'am in the most respectful way. The shooting occurred an hour ago at Ed's Burgers. The commissioner was just sitting down to have a burger and some soda on one of the outside tables. To answer your other question, the commissioner received a gunshot wound between his eyes, which killed him instantly. He's already been pronounced dead at the scene."

"Have the coroner's crew picked up his body yet?"

"No sir, they were ordered to stand down until they heard from your office and staff."

"Deputy Andros, please go to the murder scene immediately. Take this new recruit with you. Make sure that you secure the crime scene. Allie and I will be over there shortly."

"You got it Eric. To be very open, I'm very angry about this."

"Keep your head and emotions in check. Harry would've wanted that. I'm sure that we're going to find this murderer pretty quickly."

Andros grabbed his badge and side arm from Eric's desk then left the office with the new recruit following him. Allie noticed that Eric's eyes had turned completely black. Blood vessels were pulsing out of the veins in his forehead. Allie quickly grabbed the keys to the Chevy then they both left the office. She knew there was no time to waste. After they got in she started the car then revved the engine, which sounded like thunder coming from the heavens. Allie then peeled rubber out of the office building and made a bee line to Ed's Burgers.

Eric seemed very quick. His vampire nails formed on his hands. She had a worried look on her face as they pulled in to Ed's Burgers. The CSI team already were collecting evidence. Eric sent other deputies to canvass the entire area. Andros knew in his gut that a sniper was who killed Harry. Eric, Allie and Andros made sure they other deputies would give them some privacy as they viewed his body. They turned their backs to keep them out of prying eyes. With a look of anger, Andros removed the sheet from Harry's body. Tears streamed down Allie's face as she viewed Harry's body. The bullet hole between his eyes looked precise. This told them it was done by somebody with sniper or military training. It was time to use his powers to view the last few moments of Harry's life.

ERIC AND ALLIE GRABBED each of his hands. With his hands shaking, Andros placed his hand on Harry's arm. All of them closed their eyes with deep regret in their hearts. Suddenly, all of them appeared in the distance viewing Harry just receiving his burger. The look of extreme hunger came over him. *I'm hungry enough to eat the horse and chase the rider.* he chuckled to himself. The ice-cold soda seemed to be calling his name. Harry took a huge swig before taking a hulkish bite of his burger. Andros looked off in the distance using his enhanced vision as a vampire. He noticed a black van that looked like something out of the seventies. It appeared to be about sixty yards away from the restaurant. He noticed a very elderly man get out of the driver's side of the van. He pulled out a rifle then placed a scope on it. Andros noticed this man looked like a stout five foot ten and around one hundred and sixty pounds.

Using his mind, he went closer then noticed this man had a very full head of gray hair. He quickly rubbed his chin of his razor stubbled face. Andros also noticed that this man had a glass eye. He took a visual of the license plate number of the van, QXT 3762, Maine plates. A very obese young man got out of the passenger side door of the van. This man appeared to be around six feet in height with balding fire engine red hair. He looked like he ate one too many donuts in this past. Andros sized him up to be around four hundred and fifty pounds. He then turned his attention back to Harry. A loud POP! rang out from the rifle of the elderly man. Andros heard the bullet WHISP! as it made its way to toward Harry. Within seconds, the round hit Harry between his eyes. They all angrily looked as Harry died instantly. Allie noticed his mouth gaping open with a look of horror on his face. Within seconds, Harry's spirit appeared in front of them. A look of extreme anger and sadness came over Eric's face.

"I'm so angry and also very sad this happened to you Harry. Do you have any idea as to who shot you?"

"Yes, I certainly know who shot me. About six months ago, I put Ted Corten into prison for rape and attempted child molestation. He has another brother that's a former marine that served in Vietnam. He has a very obese younger brother also. I'm sure they had an ax to grind with me."

"Harry, you certainly know that I'll be able to bring you back as a vampire. You'll be able to seek justice against your murderer."

"No, I've been informed that I can't come back. It was my time to die. That is the only case that I can think of, boys."

"Does this older man have a glass eye? Does he also have a young obese brother?"

"Yeah, how did you know Andros?"

"In the distance before you were shot, I found a black van that looked to be a seventies model. A man with a glass eye shot you. I also noticed an obese younger fellow on the passenger side of the van."

"The old man is Max Corten. The younger fatter chap is Ray Corten. Please make sure the evidence you obtain is solid. Please avenge my death!"

Seconds later, the spirit of Harry slowly began to fade from them. Eric, Allie and Andros instantly teared up as he vanished from them. They broke their hold on Harry's body. Eric waved to the coroner and his crew to take the body to the examiner's office. Eric decided to send out the rest of the crew to find evidence. He also called the prosecutor's office to get search warrants and arrest warrants for Ray and Max Corten. He also decided they needed to have a meeting at their home.

Allie gladly drove them to their home in a very swift manner. She knew that they wanted to talk about a plan to avenge and solve Harry's murder. They quickly got out of the car then went inside of the house. Andros opened three ice cold cans of grape soda as they sat at the table. Eric and Allie sat down but remained quiet for the next few moments.

"The search warrants have already been granted. They emailed me a copy of them. They are blanket warrants. The arrest warrants have also been approved for them. What do you think our first move should be, Andros?"

"We need to find the black van also need to find the murder weapon. I remembered the license plate number. The DMV confirmed the black van is registered to Ray Corten. My opinion is we need to get evidence first before we arrest both of them. I think we should put out an active warrant over dispatch for getting the van. Once found, every inch of the van needs to be searched for forensic evidence. What's your take on this, old sport?"

"I just got an email on my phone. They've already impounded the van. It's on the grounds of the jail an being searched as we speak. The murder weapon is still not in our custody. It's pretty obvious this murder was premeditated. Ray Corten sought revenge on Harry for putting his brother in prison. The state of Maine doesn't sanction the death penalty but they should in his case. We'll let the wheels of justice take care of both of them."

"I think we should find the murder weapon. I'm one

hundred percent confident that the ballistics with match the slug they have already pulled out of Harry's skull, old sport."

"The search warrants should take care of that. I'm going to let our staff take care of that. We need to figure out our next move should be in this case."

"I think it would be prudent of us to first of all find both of them. Then do some surveillance on them. Once they find the murder weapon and then ballistics match. I would like Deputy Andros to immediately arrest both of them," Allie said as she took a big swig of her grape soda then give off a big, obnoxious BURP!

"Allie did you get any of that on you?"

"Why I certainly did, my darling husband."

"Andros, have you heard from any of our staff as to the whereabouts of Ray and Max Corten?"

"I've heard they took off in an old truck then drove out to the old mine on the west side of town. They got wind that we were looking for them. This is when the search warrants were issued on their residence, old sport."

"Are you talking about the decommissioned Walker mine? That place has been shut down for over forty years."

"Yes, some junior deputies were following them. Ray was able to ditch their tail but I'm confident we'll be able to find them there."

"Sounds good to me. What do you think Allie?"

"I'm in agreement, let's find those bastards!"

"I've also been informed from one of our junior deputies both the ballistics match that of the slug they pulled out of Harry's skull. The murder weapon has also been found. These two guys are a bit sloppy. It should be a cinch to arrest them, old sport."

"We are all higher ranking. All of us need to learn to delegate, however, we are talking about Harry here. Are you ready to get our butts to the area surrounding the Walker Mine?"

"You bet your ass I am. Let's get the hell out of here."

"Andros and Eric, we need to keep a cool head about this. I understand both of you are pretty angry that our dear friend and coworker Harry is dead. If we go at this with our horns down and asses up, mistakes are going to happen. Do you get what I'm saying here? Max should be our first target. He's the one that murdered Harry. His son Ray will be easy to take care of."

"Allie, I think you're right. Our approach should be concise and by the book. Harry would've wanted it that way. Do we have firearms and vests in the back of the Chevy?"

"Yes sir, we do. My gut instinct is they are hiding out at Walker Mine. Let's go boss."

"Allie, are you ready?"

"Yes, let's drive to the outskirts of Walker Mine. All of the warrants are ready to be used. Including the ones for the immediate arrest of Max and Ray Corten."

Allie took the keys out of her pocket. Eric graciously opened the driver's side door then she got in. Andros piled in the backseat. He finally got in the passenger seat. She kicked the car over then looked at Eric. The expression on her face was that of a lioness seeking out her prey after a long period of hunger. Rocks and dust went flying in several directions as she peeled out. Andros held on in the back seat for his life. Eric chuckled to himself as they approached the outskirts of Walker Copper Mine.

Andros noticed the lock to the gate was breached, which meant someone was on the property. Allie pulled inside the entrance then parked the car behind a supply shack last used over forty years ago. Andros looked around the immediate area after getting a bulletproof vest and police issued fire arm. He went left toward the entrance of the mine. Eric and Allie do the same then go to the right toward the entrance. The vampire instincts took over for Andros and Eric. They put their noses up in the air.

"Andros, do you smell human blood?"

"I do smell human blood. I wonder where it's coming from."

"While both of you smell blood, I've noticed blood droplets about two feet in front of us."

Andros quickly scurried over to Eric and Allie's location.

"Could one of them be hurt? We know that it can't be Harry's blood. He was shot from a distance. My gut tells me it's either human blood or blood of wild game."

Andros reached down then put his finger in one of the droplets. He then tasted the sample.

"What kind of blood is it, Andros?"

"It's human blood, boss. One thing that I forgot to tell you about this place. Some wild game hunters from the west coast trapped then tranquilized a couple of grizzly bears not native to this part years ago. They did this just for sport. A cruel way to treat one of God's creatures."

SUDDENLY THE HAIR ON the back of Eric's head stood on end. Andros transformed into his true vampire persona for self-preservation. The sounds of a big animal lurking in the distance came to their ears. Allie looked behind them then turned completely white at what she saw. Eric and Andros did the same. In a split second, Eric tore off his shirt then removed his pants. He screamed as his face contorted then a big snout replaced his nose. Fur and blood-soaked fangs came out of his mouth. The rest of his body then transformed in a werewolf. Saliva dripped from his lips as they turned completely around.

Two grizzly bears both stood on their back legs coldly staring at them. The smell of human flesh seemed to excite the two bears. A very big GROWL! rang out from both of them. Eric's very huge size didn't even faze the grizzlies. They were looking at them as if they were their next meal. Allie had a look of pure terror on her face as she slowly backtracked toward the car. Andros looked at Eric with his ghostly white skin a very large blood-soaked fang dripping with saliva. His eyes were completely black. They both walked slowly toward the two grizzlies. They both stood around seven feet in height. Eric sized them up to be close to eight hundred pounds each. Each of the bears got on all fours then rushed towards Andros and Eric.

The two grizzlies leaped high in the air as they made contact with them. In midair, one of the grizzlies using his razor-sharp claws took a swipe at the left arm of Andros. Blood sprayed out of his arm. Andros figured that it was his turn to cause some damage. Using his quick reflexes and his own claws he took his swipe at the bear in front of him. The head of the bear in front of him toppled to the ground. Blood shot high in the air. Andros caught a majority of the falling blood in his mouth. His eyes showed excitement. As they both landed, Andros ripped the body of the lifeless bear into shreds. Blood and sinew flew in several directions. A very big SCREAM! rang out of his lips as he peered over to Eric. What was left of the bear's body convulsed as the nervous system was taking over for this grizzly. He noticed that Eric's contact with the bear was delayed since he was back a little further from him.

Eric jumped in the air at the same time as his grizzly. The grizzly took a big swipe at his head but he ducked in midair. He thrust his hulk size werewolf arm in the center of the grizzly's chest. They both landed at the same time. The grizzly looked at Eric with an expression of complete horror on his face. A loud SCREAM! rang out from Eric's mouth as he bit into the beating and pulsating heart of the bear. The bear collapsed with his body convulsing due to the shock of losing the vital organ. He took both of his paws then tore the bear's body in half. Consuming all of his intestines and all blood and sinew of the body. He even sucked the marrow out of the leg bone of the bear. Eric looked at Andros then he looked back at him with blood dripping off each of their faces. Allie looked at both of them then said to herself, *Boys got to be boys!*

"You alright? It looks like the bear took a chunk of our arm."

"I'll be just fine. Within seconds, it's going to heal. I've just had a fresh feed."

"I hope to God nobody saw this happen. If someone discovers our true identities, you and I would be a in world of hurt."

Allie snapped her fingers. The remains of both of grizzlies vanished as if they were never there. She brought clothes for both of them. Eric transformed back into his human form. Andros did the same.

"Can we please focus on arresting Max and Ray Corten? I totally get why this happened, but both of you could have exposed your true identities to the public."

"We did it for self-preservation. Grizzlies are one of the most feared types of bears out there."

"While both of you were having your fun with the bears. Showing that your balls were bigger than theirs,

I've followed the droplets of blood. They led me to a small camper on the side of the entrance to the mine. They stopped at the entrance to the door of the camper. My guess is one of them is injured. My strong mermaid vision shows me that the younger one named Ray is the one that's hurt. It looks like one of those same grizzlies took a slice out of his belly. Max is trying to help him."

"Why didn't you just go and arrest them then call for back up and an ambulance to help Ray?"

"Do you think I'm stupid? You guys! I didn't want to expose you fighting the grizzly bears. Andros, call for backup and also an ambulance. Also, I believe your boss told you that the arrest is going to be one by you, Andros. You're not going to refuse a direct order from the chief, are you?"

"Sometimes Allie, you can be such a smart ass. But you're right on all of the comments you've just made."

Andros used his police radio and called in for backup. He and Eric cleaned up a little before the calvary arrived. Allie told them to stay in the background. Eric had to stay back with them to supervise them. She took Andros by the hand then led him to the camper. It would be his first arrest as a Bangor Police Department deputy. They both pulled their firearms. Eric instructed the medics to go in when he gave the signal. Andros decided to take the lead as they breached the door of the camper. Max fired a shotgun at Andros but was a very bad aim due to his glass eye. A loud POP! Rang out from Allie's pistol as she shot him in the leg. This forced him to drop his shot gun. He immediately put his hands up. Ray weakly tried to put his hands up to surrender to Andros an Allie.

"*Max and Ray Corten, you are under arrest for the murder of Commissioner Harry Montel. You are under arrest for first degree murder. You have the right to remain silent, if you give up that right all of what you say will be held against you in a court. You have the right to an attorney. If you can't afford an attorney, the City of Bangor Maine will appoint you one at low cost. Do you understand these rights as I've disclosed them to you?*" Deputy Andros asked with his eyes glued on Ray.

"I did it for my brother. I killed Harry to get revenge on ruining my brother's life. I don't really care what happens to me. I choose to invoke my right to an attorney and wish to remain silent."

"I also invoke my same rights," Ray said as blood trickled down from the gauze in his belly."

Allie waved in the medics. Eric swiftly walked up to the camper to look at Max and Ray Corten. The medics took Max and Ray Corten to the hospital with a full knowledge they were in police custody. Andros, Eric and Allie headed towards the Chevy. A look of pride was on Eric's face as they opened the car doors.

"How did it feel to make your first arrest and an official deputy of the Bangor Maine Police Department?"

"It felt damn good but I have to attend the academy in a couple of days. To be honest, I'm a little nervous but I'll be able to knock it out of the park."

"Allie and I are completely confident that you'll graduate from the academy with high honors."

"We've both been there. It'll be an honor to serve with you in the future."

"Both of you have a vacation coming up. What do you two have in mind for your vacation?"

"To be honest, we haven't really thought about it. I'm sure we'll come up with something that will be blissful. Our new roles in the police department have kept us pretty busy."

CHAPTER FOURTEEN "REVERSE REFLECTION"

 TWO DAYS LATER, ERIC and Allie watched Andros get into the bus to attend the police academy. They both got into the Chevy then took off for the spot where Allie used to dive. It seemed fitting for them. She peeled the tires. They stopped at a store along the way to buy some grape soda. Allie came back from the store with a big smile on her face as they took off again to their spot. Just before arriving they both got a premonition at the same time. Allie slammed on the brakes, the car gave out a loud SCREECH! as they came to a full stop.

"We both had the same thought. There is somebody in trouble about a block from here. My gut tells me that we need to investigate it. Why do you think Eric?"

"I would agree. Let's head over to the house on the right. It's a white house with a picket fence in front of it. It's early enough in the day that we could at least do a welfare check to make sure everything is good there."

"My instincts are kicking in. It has something to do with a mirror. If we stumble on a murder, let's work the case ourselves until we need assistance from the department."

Allie slowly drove to a very small house. By appearance it looked to be over a hundred years old.

The house itself appeared to be a little road weary. In several parts of the front, Eric saw the paint peeling off. Allie noticed the lawn hadn't been mowed in weeks. Eric was an expert at guessing how old the house could be. The house looked to be built around 1920. Allie noticed a 1977 Dodge Demon. The tires were flat and bald. Since they didn't have a warrant, they both got out of the car then walked up to the door. Allie decided she would be the one to knock. She knocked softly not to disturb the occupants much. There was no response. BANG! BANG! as she knocked harder on the door. They both looked at each other with concern.

"We might need a warrant."

"Eric, if we're doing a welfare check that's not necessary. I'm going to try and open the door."

"Allie, please be careful."

She slowly grabbed the handle then noticed that the door was unlocked. As she turned the handle, her eyes rolled back, then a vision appeared. Allie quickly grabbed Eric's hand.

SIX HOURS EARLIER AT this home. Eric and Allie found themselves in the living room. An elderly woman around seventy-five years sat down in her recliner with a cup of tea. She looked to be around a plump two hundred and fifty pounds. Allie guessed that she stood around five foot five. Her long gray hair flowed freely towards her waist. She turned on the television to watch some afternoon news. *Nothing seems out of place,* Eric thought to himself as they hid to avoid detection. They both noticed the front door opened quietly then a young man walked in. He looked to be around one hundred and fifty pounds. Allie noticed his greasy uncombed fire engine red hair. He stood around six foot in height. Eric noticed a look of lust towards this elderly woman. Judging by how loud she turned up the television, they surmised that she was hard of hearing or deaf all together. Allie noticed that this young man walked with a slight limp. Just before he reached the elderly woman, the vision abruptly ended.

Allie was the first to enter the home. The strong stench of dried blood wafted its way to their noses. It gave Eric the strong desire to throw up in his mouth. Suddenly, a horrific expression came over Allie's face as they walked into the living room. Eric's eyes got big when he also saw what she saw. The now deceased elderly woman was slumped over in her recliner. Eric put on some rubber gloves then moved the body to sit upright. Her eyelids were taped open. This told them that the killer wanted her to see her own death. Allie knelt down then noticed blood spatter from her throat being slit by the killer. The blood spatter shot towards the television's previous location. A big mirror had taken its place. Eric noticed the mirror appeared clean and free of blood spatter. Allie also noticed dried semen on the victim's nightgown. There was also blood in her crotch area, which told them there was a sexual assault on the deceased. Eric and Allie were very careful not to step in the large pool of blood in front of the victim.

"You do realize that we have to call in the troops, right?"

"Yes, we have to call the coroner's office to come and get the body. We also need the CSI team to come in dust for prints, get DNA and all that stuff. You and I need to see the last few moments of this poor woman's life before they get here. Allie, please make the call. I'm going back to the car to put police tape this whole horrific mess. The CSI team has a big job ahead of them. What's most horrifying is the killer made the deceased watch her own sexual assault and the slitting of her own throat. This also pisses me off. You and I were supposed to go and get some well-deserved time off."

"I know my darling husband, but in this situation duty calls. Please don't worry, you and I will enjoy some vacation time after this case is swiftly solved."

Allie called the coroner's office and the police department, then requested that the most senior detectives to please come to the murder scene. Eric quickly walked to the car then placed police tape and blocked off the parking lot. This was done only to protect the integrity of the scene. When he finished, he then walked back into the house.

"Are the troops coming to the scene?"

"You bet they are. We're in luck. While you were taping off the scene, I found the murder weapon. I bet we'll get a good set of fingerprints off the kitchen knife. The killer to me is a real idiot. He used the shower. There are clumps of semen and hair in the drain. This guy is going to be a slam dunk as far as evidence is concerned. Also, I looked around then found the purse belonging to the victim. She had a thousand dollars in one-hundred-dollar bills in her wallet, which rules out any attempt of robbery on the battery of charges against this guy."

"What's the victim's name, Allie?"

"She is Deborah L. Moore. She is a retired school teacher. The last few years of her life, she taught at a boy' s school for juvenile criminals. Her husband died about ten years ago. They have no children. Her husband served in the Korean War and was a disabled vet due to being shot in the lungs. I pulled up a search on my phone. Mrs. Moore has no family here in Bangor. They are both transplants from Boston Massachusetts."

"How long do we have until the calvary arrives?"

"We only have about twenty minutes. A whole bunch of a people are going to be all over this murder. Like bees on honey."

"It's time to do our thing."

Eric knelt down on the left side of the recliner then gently grasped Deborah's left hand. Allie knelt down then grabbed her right hand. They both closed their eyes to see the last few moments of her life.

DEBORAH SAT SIPPING ON her tea and watching the news without a care in the world. As previously witnessed. The ginger assailant quietly opened the door then walked with a limp to the kitchen and pulled the murder weapon out of one of the kitchen drawers then walked up to the assailant. Eric and Allie noticed right away that Deborah saw her killer. A huge expression of anger came over her face. She quickly turned the television off then coldly stared at the man as he limped toward her.

"William Kitchen, what the hell are you doing in my house! What's your business here. You have no right to be here!"

"Deborah, you and I have a score to settle. You didn't nothing but tease me when you worked at our school. With your fat plump body, you would flaunt your huge tits at the other students. I was molested by my own grandmother, so your age was a strong turn on for me."

"You fucking freak! You were caught fucking your family dog in front of the mirror. You belong in prison and not the school."

"Like I said, I have a score to settle with you."

William made his way with the kitchen knife drawn. He also had a baseball bat behind his back. He pulled it out the bat then struck her shoulder instantly breaking the socket on her left side. Deborah doubled over in pain. She could see an erection forming in the jeans William wore. He walked up to her then forced her to stand. He walked behind then pulled her nightgown up. She wore no underwear, which gave him quick access. He came up behind her then took all of his clothes off. He forced her to bend over. She could see a huge erection and precum dripping from his cock. William then forced himself deep inside of her pussy. Tears streamed down her cheeks as this young man continued to violate her body. His body stiffened as he shot cum inside of her body. With his cock still hard he forced himself deep inside of her ass. Blood shot all over his cock, which turned him on even more. He continued to go in and out of her ass. Deborah screamed letting him know that he was hurting her. William had the expression of *I do give a fuck* on his face as he continued to violate her ass.

When he finished, he forced Deborah to sit down. He forced his cock soiled with blood, her own shit and semen into her mouth. She instantly threw up all over his cock. William got angry then slapped her across both cheeks of her face. Tears streamed down her face as she wiped off her own puke. He laughed at her then called her a fucking fat slut. He found some scotch tape nearby then forced her eyes open. Deborah was too exhausted to fight him. She couldn't even lift her arms as her looked straight at her then went over to her right side then took the kitchen knife and slit her throat. A loud GURGLE! rang out from her body as she shot her own blood towards then television. He then moved the nearby mirror right in front of her. William forced her to watch her own death. Within a few minutes, Deborah gasped then took one her last breath then died as her body slumped over. William laughed loudly as he walked toward the shower.

The vision ended as Eric and Allie both let go of our hand. They both immediately threw up from what they had just witnessed. A very senior detective walked in right after they finished.

"You alright, chief?"

"If you'd just witnessed what we just did, you'd throw up to. Make sure all of the evidence is collected very carefully. You also need to get an arrest warrant issued right away for William Kitchen. He is the fucking shithead that just raped and murdered this poor woman."

"How did you know that it was William Kitchen created the horrific crime?"

"My wife and I have our ways of finding out."

"I'm also here by order of the mayor. You've just been promoted to Police Commissioner of Bangor Maine Police Department. This is until either you accept the role or a suitable replacement is found to fill the vacancy created by Harry's death."

"Let the mayor know that I accept the position."

"The mayor has also promoted you, Mrs. Bane. You're now our Chief of Police."

"Let the mayor know that I also accept the position."

The senior detective swore both of them in. This was to make their promotion official.

"Commissioner Bane, what are your orders boss?"

"Like I said before. Get the arrest warrant issued as soon as possible for William Kitchen. Make sure all of the evidence is collected carefully to protect the integrity of the case. Have the coroner take the body right away.

Chief Bane and I both have a knowledge that Deborah Moore was sexually assaulted both vaginally and anally. Detective, I want that bastard William Kitchen in police custody by the close of business today. Have I made myself clear to you. Do you have any questions?"

"No boss, you've made yourself abundantly clear. I've got this. You and the chief need to go home and clean up. Both of you will have a file your report at the department within two hours."

"You've got it Detective. The chief and I are out of here. This leaves you officially in charge. Make sure this gets done."

"You've got it boss. Get the hell out of here. I've got this sir."

Eric and Allie left the gruesome scene. They both hoped that that the case would resolve itself. Allie got in the driver's seat of the Chevy. She could see the look of anger in her husband's eyes. He opened his window to let some cool air hit his face. They decided to drive to the spot where she did her first dive as a mermaid. It seemed to be a good place to help change their current state of mind. She pulled up then they both got out of the car. Eric inhaled a big breath of the fresh air of Bangor Maine.

"It seems only fitting that we take a dive. What do you say my husband?"

"I couldn't agree more. It'll take our minds off of reality for a little while.

Suddenly, Eric's cell phone rang. Allie could see the

look of regret on his face.

"Commissioner Bane here, how can I help you?"

"Hey boss, this is Allen Thayne. One of your most senior detectives. Do you remember me?"

"Yeah, I know of you. That still doesn't explain why are you disturbing the chief and I right now."

"You've put Detective Otterman in charge of the William Kitchen matter."

"Yeah, so what Detective Thayne. You'd better get to your point. Also realize who you are talking to. I'm your police commissioner and I can strip you of your shield if you're not careful detective. So, in other words, get to the fucking point."

"No disrespect sir. William Kitchen has just committed another murder. The wife of a pastor of a highly respected Christian church's body has just been found in the City of Bangor Maine was just found?"

"How do you know it's tied to William Kitchen?"

"His prints were found on the bloody knife found at the scene. His prints were found from a very old conviction that happened about ten years ago. For some reason, a judge had the records sealed but the only access we have is his prints. No information is available about the prior case. Also, Detective Otterman put a rush on all the evidence at the murder scene that you and the chief just left from. Surprisingly, William Kitchen's DNA is also already on file. They are a one hundred percent match to the evidence found."

"I've ordered Detective Otterman to get this bastard behind bars. What the bloody hell is going on. This prick has been a very busy boy. What's the address of the new murder?"

"Sir, the address is Thirty-five Zero Seven Oxnard Lane. It's over by the old high school that they just shut down a couple of years ago. What are your orders, sir?"

"Please close off the murder scene. The chief and I will drive there. Make sure every bit of evidence is obtained by the book. I'm going to email the judge and get all the necessary warrants for search approved right away. What's the victim's name?"

"Sir, her name is Patty Jacobs. Her husband is Peter Jacobs. He's the pastor of the Home of Angels Christian church here in Bangor."

"Have you guys questioned him yet?"

"Detective Otterman has already questioned him. He's been put into protective custody until they arrest William Kitchen."

"We're driving down there now. Allie and I will take charge of the scene. Get some of your junior staff to keep looking for him."

"OK you've got it. I'm going to stay here until both of you arrive."

"Sounds good to me Detective Thayne."

Eric ended the call then quickly sent an email to the judge requesting immediate warrants to be issued on the new Jacob's case from his phone.

"I'm sure you already know what's going on. We need to get out butts down to the new murder scene."

"Yes, I totally get it Eric. After all, I'm the new chief of police and you're the new police commissioner for Bangor. Duty calls, let's get out of here."

Allie walked back to the car with Eric following closely behind her. Being the gentlemen that he was, he opened the door then she got into the driver's seat of the Chevy. He quickly got in then she fired the car over. Allie had a slight smile as she listened to the car purr like a kitten that just finished its milk. Driving like greased lighting as if the devil was chasing them. They pulled into 3507 Oxnard Lane in just mere minutes. A tall and lanky young man was there to greet them. He looked to be around six feet five in height and around a very lean one hundred and fifty pounds. Allie noticed his long blond hair, which was in a tight ponytail in the back of his head. His eyes were as blue as any ocean. Detective Thayne lifted the police tape to give them immediate access to the body. Eric told him to make sure that they were not to be disturbed as they wanted some time along with the body. After everyone was shooed away from the bedroom.

THEY FOUND A WOMAN sitting up on her bed. A nail gun was used to nail her hands to the wall on each side. Allie clearly noticed her throat was sliced going from left to right. All of her nude body was caked with dry blood. Eric noticed that a pencil had been shoved into each of her ears. Blood still trickled out of each ear.

Allie took a small light then noticed that each of her breasts had bite marks on each side. Eric also shined his flashlight onto the lower stomach and noticed dried semen on the body. Patty's mouth was gaping open and her eyes were looking straight forward. Eric and Allie both turned around only to find a huge mirror. The killer had forced her to witness her own death. This showed them that William Kitchen also had a score to settle with Patty Jacobs. She also was plump and rotund. Allie surmised that she weighed close to four hundred and fifty pounds. She pickup a bra from the floor. Allie looked at the size on the bra, fifty-five EEE. That was huge for any woman to have to deal with. Allie and Eric looked at each other then knew they needed to see the last moments of Patty Jacob's life.

Eric knelt on the left side of Patty's body. Allie knelt on the right side. They both gently grabbed her hand then close their eyes. They appeared hours earlier at the Jacob's residence. Peter Jacobs was at the church preparing for the next sermon. Patty decided it was time to spend a few moments and enjoy her alone time. She walked into the bedroom then took her bra and panties off to enjoy a cup of tea in bed. Her big breasts fell free but her nipples got hard due to the cool breeze that came out of her window.

William Kitchen knew that her husband was gone from the residence. He snuck in easily in through the door of the kitchen. Walking lightly like a thief in the night, he made his way to the bedroom. William noticed that Patty was looking at a dirty magazine. She never told her husband but she also like females. He heard a small whimper from her as he watched her rub her pussy to the picture in the magazine. This naturally turned him on. He took his clothes off then begun his voyeuristic tendencies toward her. He masturbated slowly. Just before, she was about to orgasm she noticed him standing there stroking his cock at her.

"William Kitchen, what the hell are you doing in my bedroom. You really are a sexual deviant, get the fuck out of here you pervert!"

"No way, you and I have a score to settle. You had a lesbian relationship with my own mother. This caused my parents to divorce. You're a home wrecker, you fat bitch!"

"That's where you're wrong. Your mother and I are just two woman that craved the touch of a woman. We were simply two consenting adults. That has nothing to do with why are in my bedroom and invading my privacy. What are your intentions towards me, young man?"

"I intend to get off then I'm going to make you witness your own death. You had no right to interfere with my mother and father."

Eric picked up the nail gun he brought with him. He forced her left hand to the head board then shot the nail gun into her hand. A loud CRACK! came from the nail gun as she screamed in pain. William repeated the same action on her right hand. He made sure the nail was in all the way. Patty struggled but didn't have the strength of break herself free.

He then got into her bed and sucked her left nipple. This made her skin crawl then he bit into the same breast then continued the same action on her right breast. A loud SCREAM! came out from her as she continued to struggle and watch his every move. He stroked his hard erect cock as he stood there and looked at her with a smile of murderous lust and revenge. A few moments later, he shot hot cum all over her belly. He then got on top of her then used a kitchen knife to slice her throat from left to right. Laughing wildly, he moved away from her as she watched her throat gush from blood spurting out. William Kitchen quickly put his clothes on then swiftly left the Jacob's residence. A loud GURGLE! came from her lips as she watched herself die a horrible death.

Eric and Allie let go of her hands then looked at each other with extreme sadness. A tear streamed down her face.

"This bastard deserves the same thing. You and I need to let the wheels of justice do their thing. Let's let Detective Thayne close down this up. Let's go and find this creep and get him under arrest."

"Eric, I just got an email from the department. They've realized that William Kitchen's family owns a small yacht on the northern side of Bangor. The junior detectives followed him to the marina. They've noticed that he's shopping at the little grocery store close to the marina. They are awaiting your orders, boss."

"There is no time to drive there. Please grab my hand."

ELVIS NOBLE

Eric snapped his fingers then both of them vanished from their current location. They reappeared on the dock of the marina. They both noticed a small yacht with the name of Kitchen Paradise painted on it. They also noticed that there was nobody aboard so this would be their chance. They quickly got inside then hid inside of the captain's cabin. A few moments later, they noticed William Kitchen push a huge cart of groceries toward his family's yacht. He looked left then right then brought all of the food and supplies on to the yacht. He had no knowledge of them being there. He walked with a slight limp as he reached into the outdoor refrigerator then pulled out an ice-cold beer. After taking a big gulp of his beer, he gave off a big obnoxious BURP! Eric and Allie pulled out their firearms then walked towards William. He immediately grabbed a spear gun then pointed it toward them. Allie jumped up then kicked the spear gun out of his hand. She then kneed him in the balls making him double over as if he swallowed his own balls. Eric threw the cuffs toward Allie. He wanted her to arrest him. She quickly put his arms behind his back then put the handcuffs on him.

"William Kitchen, you are under arrest for the rape and murder of Patty Jacobs and Deborah Moore. You have the right to remain silent, if you give up that right all of what you say will be held against you in a court. You have the right to an attorney. If you can't afford an attorney, the City of Bangor Maine will appoint you one at low cost. Do you understand these rights as I've disclosed them to you?"

"I have nothing to say. I know my rights. I'll be out of jail before the ink dries on any paperwork. My family has a high-powered attorney on retainer."

"Get this piece of human shit out of here, Detective Thayne. The chief and I owe you a debt of gratitude for all of your hard work on getting this piece of shit off the streets."

Eric and Allie snapped their fingers then reappeared back at the Chevy. Detective Thayne took care of the closing of the two murder cases. Allie noticed an expression of relief on her husband's face. They got into the Chevy then drove to their spot. She put the pedal to the metal. Leaving the aftermath of all the macabre and chaos behind them. Allie pulled over then got out of the driver's side and found a tree stump to sit on. Eric decided it was time to surprise her. He got in the trunk then pulled out a 1990 vintage bottle of white wine. Thinking outside the box, he reached into the cooler then pulled out two chilled wine glasses. Eric gently walked toward her. He popped the cork then poured them both a glass of wine.

"You and I have worked a hell of a lot of hours. We've not been able to spend any good quality time together. We need to enjoy the benefits of being married. I love you with all of my heart. I have an idea as how we can enjoy and celebrate our marriage."

"What do you have in mind Eric?"

"In his last will, Harry willed his own yacht to us in the event of his death. Why don't you and I take a trip on our new yacht. We could turn the cell phones off and only use the radio in case of emergency. We don't need to pack any food. We can fly off the yacht and get me blood when I need it. We can also fly and get livestock to also feed the werewolf that dwells inside of me. You and I will have the ocean to replenish ourselves. You see the setup will be just perfect for us. What do you think?"

"It sounds heavenly to me but what else do you have in mind my husband?"

"We haven't made much love due to the horrendous hours and responsibilities because of our jobs. One thing that I guarantee you that you won't be getting some sleep at least for the couple of days."

"I guess you're just going to find out how much sleep you're going to get," she said with a very seductive look on her face.

"So, do you I smell a challenge!"

Allie smiled as they enjoyed the glass of wine. She could see that Eric had finally relaxed and let go of the anger and sadness that built up due to Harry's passing. Also, the case load would be enough to get anybody down. They walked back to the car then decided to drive to the house and pack. She fired up the Chevy then revved the engine just to hear it purr like a satisfied kitten after having its milk. Eric smiled as she peeled out, only leaving dust in the wake. Twenty minutes, later they made it back home. In a mad rush, they packed a bunch of clothes and toiletries then took off to the marina. Eric had the yacht rebranded and painted with the name USS Bane on the hull.

They pulled into the marina only to find some friends had prepped the yacht and made sure it was good to go. As an added bonus, the marina staff placed a table on the main deck of the yacht. In his will, Harry wanted to make sure on their first maiden voyage that they would celebrate with some vintage cognac and also a four-thousand-dollar bottle of white wine. The staff fulfilled their promise to Harry.

Both Eric and Allie grabbed their luggage then headed to the yacht with huge smiles on their faces. The rebranded yacht in the darkness of the night gleamed as if it were a beacon of hope and peace. As the walked up the brow, Allie caught Eric looking at the waves of the ocean giving off a fury with the evening tide. She smiled at him to let him know that she felt very happy. Just before they made it to the table, the yacht staff grabbed their luggage and took it to their huge bedroom.

"Have you decided where you want to go, Eric?"

"To be honest, I haven't put a lot of thought into it. It doesn't really matter as long as we both enjoy ourselves. Also, that I'm with you. Not saving the world from itself will give us some peace."

"I think that we should cruise out about twenty miles then drop anchor. That will put us close to everything. You and I will be close to everything. How does that sound?"

"Sounds good to me. Let's have a stiff shot of cognac to commemorate our maiden voyage of the USS Bane."

The gracious staff already warmed up the cognac then poured a shot for both of them. Eric popped the cork for them to enjoy the wine. She looked at him as if he was her next meal. Her eyes symbolized as a window to the heavens. They both enjoyed the shot of cognac, which warmed their bodies on such a cold night. Eric took Allie by the hand then they walked out to look at the ocean.

In the distance, they saw the old lighthouse, giving off its signals to approaching vessels. A small but powerful green light did its duty. The moon was shining brightly across the water, an orange color, which looked spectacular. Eric grabbed her hand then squeezed it tightly as he moved over to passionately kiss her. When their lips met, it was like a huge dormant volcano getting ready to erupt.

"What's next for us Eric?"

"Only time will tell my love."

The End

ABOUT THE AUTHOR

ELVIS NOBLE

Elvis Noble is not your prototypical crime solving horror or suspense writer. His books transcend into several genres. The stories he writes take on split personalities. There is a little of everything in his work. Mr. Noble's writings are best described as an X File story with a C.S.I. twist. The thrill is in the chase. He takes the readers of his work on a spine-tingling, mind-boggling and unpredictable trip. The plots in his stories provide readers with diverse details, mixing modern day techniques with surreal fictional accounts of the unknown. The pages of his stories carry a flavor of mythology, time travel, lust and love, blood and gore, sorrow and happiness, innocence and immortality. If a reader likes to be on the edge of their seat wondering what will happen next, then his writing is a good fit for readers. He possesses a quick hitting writing style that is short on dialogue but long on action. His works are quick, direct and decisive where good prevails over evil.

Elvis Noble is accredited with writing prolific books such as Redemption, The Lost Souls Book One (2008), Deliverance, The Lost Souls Book Two (2008), Hell's Gate (2008), Hell's Gate Book Two (2011), Canadian Mayhem, The Lost Souls Book Three (2011). He served as an editor and promotional director for seven years, which qualifies him to write and deliver a masterfully written story to the clamoring and avid readers out there. He resides in the Pacific Northwest and enjoys the love of his craft. Elvis enjoys sharing his vivid imagination with the world.